celg

MAR 2 3 2021.

LUCK
AND A
HORSE

Center Point
Large Print

Also by Max Brand® and available from
Center Point Large Print:

Gunfighters in Hell
Sunset Wins
The Double Rider
Stagecoach
Magic Gun
The White Streak
The Wolf and the Man
The Tracker
Rodeo Ranch

**This Large Print Book carries the
Seal of Approval of N.A.V.H.**

LUCK AND A HORSE

A Western Duo

Max Brand®

CENTER POINT LARGE PRINT
THORNDIKE, MAINE

This Circle Ⓥ Western is published by
Center Point Large Print in the year 2021 in
co-operation with Golden West Literary Agency.

First Edition
February 2021

The name Max Brand® is a registered trademark with the
United States Patent and Trademark Office and cannot be
used for any purpose without express written permission.

Printed in the United States of America
on permanent paper.
Set in 16-point Times New Roman type.

ISBN: 978-1-64358-814-8

The Library of Congress has cataloged this record
under Library of Congress Control Number: 2020948321

EDITOR'S NOTE

These two stories were found in a cache of previously unpublished stories—mostly non-Westerns. It is hard to imagine why they were passed up by any pulp magazine editor those many years ago in that they are both marvelous stories. We're happy that they are finally being made available for fans of Max Brand Westerns.

TRAYNOR

I

The place looked safe and it felt safe. The stagecoach had come in sight of its destination at Little Snake. The passengers could wipe the dust from their faces and see the wriggle and flash of the river that crossed the flat and split the town in two. That tremendous sun of the western summer helped to give a sense of drowsy peace. The mountains themselves were rather dreamlike than mighty. Heat waves dimmed them and the strata of vari-colored rocks made the range like one of those stippled atmospheric effects in a modern painting. Altogether, it was a scene to induce sleep, and the passengers could not help yearning toward the cool, dark shadows under the pine trees.

Young Larry Traynor, in the driver's seat, knotted his brows a little as he prepared to sweep the stage down the cataracting slopes that led into the flat below. Certainly, there was no thought of danger in his mind. He had a good set of brakes whose lining was his own work, and he had a pair of excellent leaders. Six months ago those buckskins had come into his hands as raw as bar whiskey. Now they were as smooth as an old blend. He hardly needed the long reins of them. His voice was enough, and they pulled wide or close according to the curves they encountered. Besides, when Larry Traynor came in view of Little Snake something moved like music in his blood, a happy sadness as he thought of Rose Laymon. Once she had been close to him. Time and another man had put a distance between them and now there was only the melancholy beauty of daydreams and memories such as those which now floated up between him and the white glare of the road.

The stage was rolling over the last of the upgrade. It lurched onto the level. Traces and chains loosened. Traynor was about to call to the leaders when a voice barked from a clump of brush inside the curve of the road. The sound of that voice, shrill and piercing, scattered the sleepy unreality of the moment. A long rifle barrel gleamed through the bushes. A masked head rose to view—sleek black cloth with white showing through the eye slits. Some monster of the antediluvian ages might have risen like this, hunting for prey.

Sam Whitney, the veteran guard who shared the driver's seat with Traynor, muttered—"The damned rat"—and jerked up the double-barreled, sawed-off shotgun which was always under his hand.

He got halfway up from his seat before the rifle spoke. There was no flame, no smoke—just the shiver of the barrel and the clanging noise. Sam

Whitney kept on leaning forward. He threw the rifle before him. He fell from the seat as the stagecoach lurched to a stop under the brakes which Traynor had thrown on.

Traynor saw the body of his old friend hit the rump of the off-wheeler. He saw a spray of blood fly. Then, Whitney, turning in the air, landed with a solid impact in the road. The dust exploded outward from the blow. Sam Whitney lay still, flat on his back, and looked with thoughtful eyes at the glare of the afternoon sky.

Traynor could only see that picture. He hardly heard the shrill voice that commanded the passengers out of the coach. It was a strange voice, too high and sharp to be real. Only something in the subconscious mind of Traynor kept his hands stretched high above his head. Vaguely he was aware that the passengers had their arms high over their heads, also, and that one man was obeying the commands of the robber to throw things out of the boot.

There was money back there. More than twenty thousand dollars.

The robber was cursing the silent men who faced him in a line. He held his rifle under the hollow of his arm while he accepted the canvas sack in his other hand. If they tried to follow him, they would catch hell, the masked man was saying. Then he was backing up into the brush. The sun glinted for the last time on the rifle. The

11

green leaves swayed together. The fellow was gone.

And still Traynor sat for a rigid moment with his arms stuck up high above his head. His heart had leaped up into his throat and trembled there, beating too fast for a count. For the last three months, whenever a moment of excitement came, his heart acted like that, paralyzing his body.

Nerves, he thought to himself. *The old woman in me is coming out.*

But suddenly he could move, he could realize.

He sprang down into the road and kneeled in the dust.

"Sam! Hey! Sam!" he called.

Out of the Babel of voices of men congratulating one another that the robber had not stripped them of watches and wallets, Traynor heard a fellow saying: "He killed the guard, all right."

"Almighty God!" said Traynor.

He could not believe it. Dead men should stare at the world with dead eyes. But there was still the old twinkle of humor in the look of Sam Whitney. Just as when he stood at a bar, resting one foot on the rail, hurrying through an anecdote before he swallowed his drink. He looked on the verge of making some humorous retort to the last speaker.

"Possums taught me how to play dead," he would say.

But he said nothing. His eyes would not move from the distance into which they peered. And there was a great red splotch across his breast.

"It's true," said Traynor, and ran for the buckskin leaders.

He had a revolver with him. Fool that he was, he could remember now that he was armed.

He cut the near leader out of its harness, leaped on the bare back, and raced the horse into the brush, up the slope. His passengers howled after him. Their voices were no more to Traynor than sounds of the journeying wind.

Sam Whitney was dead! And there never would be peace in Traynor's soul until the murderer went down.

Old Sam Whitney had taught him how to throw a rope.

Old Sam Whitney—why, he had always been old, even when Traynor was only a child. He had taught Traynor how to thrum a guitar. And how to shoot. And how to stick to the back of a pitching bronco.

"If you're feeling sick, maybe that damned mustang will be feeling a lot sicker," Sam Whitney used to say.

He taught Traynor how to fight. "The other fellow looks good when he's hitting, but he looks damned bad when he's being hit. Bulldog, bulldog is the trick."

Sam Whitney was dead but part of his soul

would live on in the minds of his friends, in the mind of Larry Traynor above all.

Bulldog . . . that was the thing. . . .

The buckskin, running like a racer, blackened with sweat already, streaked across the round forehead of the mountain, through trees, into the clear. And yonder galloped a big man on a swift little horse, a quick-footed little sorrel, pretty as a picture and active as a cat.

A mountain man on a mountain horse, no doubt.

The robber turned the blank mask of his face with the beastly white showing through the eye holes. He snatched up his rifle. And Traynor, as the buckskin ran in, fired twice.

The first bullet hit empty air, and he knew it. The second shot skidded the sombrero off the head of the robber. Then the rifle spoke and the buckskin fell on its nose.

Traynor turned a somersault, got staggering to his feet, and fired once more at a dim vision which was disappearing through the thick of the brush. The only answer that came back to him was the clattering of hoofs that disappeared into the distance.

He turned to the buckskin. The bullet had clipped it right between the eyes—beautiful shooting! Shooting almost too beautiful, because there were not half a dozen men in the mountains who were able to make a snap shot as effective as this. Such accuracy narrowed the field in which he would have to search.

Perhaps, after all, it would not take half a lifetime to bring the murderer to justice!

He stripped the bridle and harness from the poor, limp, dead thing. The buckskin looked sleek and small. It looked like a mere colt now that the fire of life had been snuffed out of it. But what a prince among horses it had seemed when it danced and pranced into a station with the foam flecking its chest and neck and shoulders!

Traynor went over to the spot where the sombrero had fallen. It was a Stetson. There are thousands of Stetsons through the West. Who could identify a man through his Stetson?

He looked at the sweat band, where initials of owners are often punctured through the leather, but there was no sign. The hat was new, which made it all the worse as an identifying mark.

He tried it on his head. It was a perfect fit, and that made him sigh with a greater despair.

However, he had something to go on. A mountain man riding a sorrel mountain horse, an active little beauty. A fellow who was a dead shot.

Or had that bullet been intended for the breast of Traynor when the tossing head of the mustang intercepted its course? As well be hunted for two murders as for one.

Thoughtfully, Traynor walked over the round of

the slope and back into the road. The passengers started clattering at him. At least they had had the decency to put the dead body of Sam Whitney back into the coach. Someone had closed his eyes. He looked like one asleep.

"No luck," said Traynor gloomily. "This hat . . . and that's all."

He put the other buckskin leader behind the stage and drove down the sloping road with only four horses, the pointers acting bewildered when they found themselves at the head of the team.

They were entering Little Snake. A crowd, half mounted and half running on foot, was already trailing about the stagecoach, shouting questions when the fattest and oldest man among the passengers called: "There's Bill Clancy's clothing store! Stop over there and see if he might have sold this hat."

It was a small hope but it was better than nothing, so Traynor stopped the coach. The crowd fell on the passengers. Half a dozen attached themselves to each man, babbling questions, getting terse, important answers. Not every man has the importance of stage robbery hitched to his experience. These fellows made the most of their situation.

When they got into Clancy's store, they stood first at the counter with proprietorial airs, waiting for Clancy to finish examining the hat.

He was a sour-faced little man, this Clancy, but he set for the town certain fashions in silk neckties and neatly fitted clothes and pearl gray hats that made him respected, almost a superior citizen.

Now he took the Stetson on the tip of his finger and caused it to rotate slowly under his eyes. His hands were pale, clean, delicately shaped. He had the air of an artist examining a mystery, and a beautiful mystery, at that.

He turned the hat over, regarded the sweat band, which was only slightly darkened toward the front.

"The gentleman who wore this hat," pronounced Mr. Clancy, "did not sweat a whole lot around the forehead."

He turned down the leather sweat band and looked inside it.

"Gentlemen," he said, "I sold this hat."

There was a little grunting sound from the whole crowd, as if they had all been in a conveyance and had gone over a jolting bump. Traynor began to feel cold about the lips.

"I sold this hat," Clancy said, "and the name of the gentleman to whom I sold it was . . ." He paused, studying something that caught his attention. "I always write in the initials of the purchaser," murmured Clancy, in the midst of his thought. "These initials are rubbed a little dim . . . but . . . yes . . . this is the hat that I sold to Doctor

17

Parker Channing three weeks ago on Tuesday."

No one spoke. There were good reasons for the silence. Sleek and handsome young Parker Channing had come to Little Snake three months ago on his way to the mountains for a shooting trip. But he found a dozen cases suddenly ready for him and not another physician within fifty miles to rival him.

He lingered to do his professional duty, and then he settled down for an indefinite stay. His reputation was carried on the wings of the wind. When he operated on the skull of Tim Wallace and saved either Tim's life or reason, or both, by removing a segment of the bone, his skill as a surgeon was established. And when he saved the wife of Big Joe Mellick from death by typhoid, it was apparent that he was an excellent medical man, also. If his prices were high, his services were worth it.

He became at one stride the leading professional man of the town. He was an honor to it. He could stick to the back of a bucking mustang as well as the next fellow. He could shoot circles around nearly every man in the district when it came to a hunting party. He was the best of company, had a tight head to hold whiskey, and, in a word, was such an all-around prize that it was little wonder that he took the eye of the prettiest girl in town. He walked her away from Larry Traynor the very first time he met her.

And that was why most heads in the Clancy store now turned suddenly toward Traynor— not because it was his dear friend who had been murdered, but because it was apparent that Dr. Channing was the murderer.

Clancy could not fail to rise to a situation of this magnitude. He leaned across the counter and offered the Stetson to Traynor.

"I guess you'll be wanting to give this hat back to the gent that owns it, Larry."

Give it back to the handsome doctor? Perhaps receive some lead out of the doctor's gun in exchange?

Traynor accepted the dangerous mission with his eyes on the floor. His heart was up there in his throat again. He could not move; he could not speak. A strange, dizzy sense of faintness was sickening him.

Then he thought of the dead man and lifted his head suddenly.

"I'll look up Doctor Channing," he said.

II

The stagecoach had to be taken to the station. The passengers left the Clancy store with Traynor, and he drove at a dog-trot back to headquarters.

Abe Terry, the general manager of the line, sat on the waiting bench in front of the station stable, whittling a stick and spitting tobacco juice into the deep dust of the street.

He did not move to avoid the cloud of white dust that blew over him. He merely lifted his head a little to watch the men who took off their hats before they carried the dead man into the building. He was whittling again and working at his quid when Traynor came up to him.

"Yeah, I've heard," said Abe Terry. "Gonna go and have a chat with the doctor?"

"I'm going to go and have a chat with him," agreed Traynor.

"He'll shoot hell right out of you," said Abe thoughtfully.

"Yeah, maybe he will."

"It's your party," said Abe, "but why not wait till the sheriff gets in? He's due sometime this afternoon."

"If I can find the doctor, I'm going to have it out with him," said Traynor.

"Are you?" asked Abe, looking up quickly.

21

"That's what I want to do."

"Well, more power to you. Watch both his hands. The sucker is ambidextrous, they tell me."

"I've got to find him, first."

"That ain't any trouble. Over at the Laymon house . . . he's out on the front porch, chewin' the fat with Rose."

Traynor nodded, reaching into his pocket. "Supposing that anything happened," he said. "Put this ten bucks on old Sam, will you?"

Abe Terry took the greenback and rubbed it between his fingers.

"What the hell good will ten bucks do Sam now?" he asked.

"Flowers, or something," said Traynor.

"Yeah. Flowers or . . . what the hell?"

"Turn it into coffee and meat, or whiskey for the drunks that are broke," said Traynor. "It comes from Sam. That's all."

"Owe him this?" asked Abe.

"More than that. I owe Sam millions."

"Oh, that's the way, is it?" asked Terry. And he spat into the dust again. "Fond of the old goat, were you? Look here, Larry. Why be a damned fool? Why not wait till the sheriff gets home?"

"If I were the fellow that lay cold," said Traynor, "Sam wouldn't wait for any sheriff."

"Well, go on and play your hand," said Abe Terry. "I'm wishing you luck. Remember if you start shooting from the hip, you're likely to pull to the right. I always noticed that. I pulled a gun on a Canuck down in Flaherty's saloon, once, and I shot a bottle off the bar right beside his left arm. Then he put a dose of lead inside my hip and turned me into a lame duck for the rest of my life."

He waved his hand. "So long, Larry."

"So long, Abe."

The Stetson was still in the hand of Traynor. As though it were a flag, it called people toward it. There were half a hundred men and boys walking around the block after him toward the Laymon house.

The men sauntered at ease, each fellow pretending that his way simply happened to coincide with that of Traynor's. But they kept advising the boys to get back out of the way of possible trouble. It came over Traynor that he would certainly be left alone to start the trouble with the doctor. The crowd would hold back.

Not that the men were cowards. There in Little Snake lived as many brave fellows as one could wish to see, but Traynor had a special purpose in enforcing this arrest and the crowd would hold back and let him make his try. If he failed—well, even then nothing might be done. The law ought to take care of its own troubles, and the sheriff was the law in Little Snake.

The Laymon house hove in view. It was two

tall stories high and had a whole block of trees and garden around it. John Laymon never did things by halves. Thirty miles out from town he had one of the best ranches in the valley, crowded with fat cattle. But he preferred to keep his family closer to the stage line. Money had come to John Laymon through his patient labor and keen brain. Reputation had come to him some three or four years ago when he had rounded up the entire Wharton gang of rustlers who had been preying on the cattle of the community. He had brought in the sheriff, raised a force of fighting cowpunchers, contributed his own wise head and steady hand, and they had scooped up the gang and sent the Whartons to prison. After that, John Laymon spent less of his time on his distant ranch which lay back among the mountains in a fertile valley. He was more often in town.

But he was not in sight as Traynor advanced toward the house. There was only Rose Laymon in a white dress—and the doctor.

Her arms were bare. Her throat was bare. She was as brown as a schoolboy, and Traynor could guess at the blue of her eyes long before he could see the color, actually.

She was small and slender, but her wrists and her arms and her throat were rounded. Traynor could see the flash of her laughter from the distance, and then he turned in up the path, under the big shade trees.

The crowd waited behind him. Some of the men leaned on the fence. Some remained clear across the street. It was a big, wide, naked street. One day the people of Little Snake intended to plant trees on each side and make the thoroughfare a boulevard, but that was a dream which had not been realized.

The soul of Traynor felt as big and wide and desolate as the street when he turned up the path, carrying the white Stetson. For the town was looking on, not taking part. Little Snake wanted to see a show, and Traynor was merely to be on the stage.

The doctor lounged in a chair near the girl. He wore gray flannel pants and a white shirt open at the throat, without a necktie. There was no other man in Little Snake who would have dared to wear such clothes—not even Clancy himself. But the doctor had no fear. He wore white shoes, also, and he had his legs crossed and swung one little foot up and down.

When he saw Traynor coming with the hat, however, he began to straighten himself in his chair, little by little. He was big and he was lean; he was supple and quick. He had the look of a fellow who might be capable of almost any physical exertion, and as a matter of fact he was as good as his looks.

But what depressed Traynor more than all else was the great sweep of the intellectual

brow above that handsome face. The doctor
had everything from education to brains. It was
not at all strange that he had taken Rose away
from Traynor at a gesture. What was Traynor in
comparison but a rather stodgy figure, a common
cowpuncher not even distinguished for skill with
a rope or a branding iron?

He was merely "one of us" and people like the
doctor always ride herd on the ordinary man.
The immensity of the gulf between him and the
murderer kept widening in the understanding of
Traynor as he drew closer. He could see himself
as a mere pawn contrasted with a king among
men. It seemed to him miraculous that he, Larry
Traynor, could ever have sat on that verandah, as
on a royal dais, at the side of Rose Laymon.

He went up the front stops, one at a time,
tipping his hat to the girl. He took his hat clear
off. Sweat began to run on his hot forehead. He
raised his left arm and wiped the sweat off on the
flannel sleeve of his shirt.

The girl stood before him, saying coldly: "Do
you want something . . . Larry?"

She had started to say "mister" and then shame,
perhaps, had stopped her. But he could forgive
pride in such a girl. Let the pretty woman pick
and choose because once they have chosen, they
settle down to trouble enough.

"I want to give this hat back to the doctor," said
Larry.

He offered it, with a gesture.

Parker Channing sat forward, rose. He took the hat in a careless hand, examined it.

"I never saw it before," he said.

"No?" said Traynor. His heart was beginning to rise in his breast, stifling him.

"No, I never saw it before," said the doctor.

"What's this all about?" asked the girl. "Why do you look at Parker with such a terrible eye, Larry?"

"Because I was wondering," breathed Traynor. "I was wondering whether or not he was a murderer."

The girl made two or three quick steps back. She put out a slim hand against the wall of the house. The heat had crumpled the white paint to roughness.

"Don't pay any attention, Parker," she said. "He's simply drunk again."

That was the way she had been talking to the doctor about him, then? A town drunkard—was that what she had been making of him?

"I won't pay too much attention to him," said the doctor. "He's not drunk . . . though he looks a bit like it."

And his gaze suddenly narrowed, became professionally curious. It fastened like teeth on the throat of Traynor. A malicious interest gleamed in his eyes.

What does he see? Traynor asked himself.

"A man wearing this hat," said Traynor, "held up the stage I was driving and shot old Sam to death."

"Not Sam!" cried the girl. "Larry, not old Sam!"

"Yes . . . and he's dead."

"But he can't be! Only two days ago . . ."

She stopped. Something was passing between the two men that locked up her speech in ice.

"The murderer was wearing this hat. You never saw the hat before, Doctor?"

"Never," said Channing. "Sorry to hear about . . ."

"You're sorry, are you?" muttered Traynor. There was rage in him to warm his blood, but always there was that horrible fluttering of his heart, and the need to gape wider for air.

"You never even saw this Stetson before?"

"I've told you before, man. What's the matter with you?" asked Parker Channing coldly.

"Your initials are inside the sweat band, where Clancy wrote them in when he sold you this three weeks ago on Tuesday."

The doctor's head jerked back. His right hand darted inside his coat.

"No, Parker!" cried the girl. "No, no!"

Traynor's grip was on the butt of his Colt. He did not draw it. There seemed no strength in him to draw the gun. He knew, by the cold of his face, that he was deadly white. His eyes ached. They thrust out so hard. And there came over him the frightful surety that he was a coward.

He could not believe it. He has gone through his troubles—not many of them, but he had faced what all Westerners have to face—half-mad horses under the saddle, high, dangerous trails, and sometimes an argument with an armed drunkard in a saloon. Yet here he found himself hardly able to breathe, and the tremor from his heart had invaded his entire body.

"You don't mean that he's right," moaned Rose Laymon. "It's not really your hat, Parker?"

The doctor, breathing hard, swayed a little back and shook his head.

"No . . . not mine. At least . . . if it's mine, then someone else stole it. I don't know anything about . . . the murder. . . ."

He was always as cool as steel. But now the coolness was gone. The guilt withered and puckered his face, narrowed his eyes. What was he seeing, briefly, in the distance of time? All the high promise of his life was falling in ruins, of course. And in the presence of the girl he had wanted to marry.

"Ah, damn your rotten heart!" said the doctor, and walked straight up to Traynor.

It was the time to stand on guard, but the arms of Traynor were lead. The figures before him shifted, were raised from their places, wavered in the thin air. The brightness of the sun was gone. He could no longer feel the beating of his heart. His lungs labored, but the life-given air would not enter them, it seemed. He could hear a rasping, quick pulse of sound and knew that it came out of his own throat.

The doctor struck him across the face and leaped back half a step, his hand inside his coat, half crouched, perfectly on edge to make the draw.

"You lying dog!" Dr. Channing thundered.

And Traynor could not move.

"How horrible," he heard the girl whisper.

And, far away on the street, where the men of the town were watching, he heard a deep, steady groaning noise. Nothing as shameful as this had ever been seen in Little Snake.

Cowards have been known to faint in a crisis. And Traynor wanted to faint; he wanted to lie down on the flat of his back and close his eyes and concentrate on the frightful problem of getting enough air into his lungs. Instead, he had to stand, like a wretched, crumbling statue.

The girl walked between him and Channing.

"Don't touch him again," she said scornfully. "Whatever you are . . . whatever you've done, Parker, you don't strike a helpless coward a second time."

"Certainly not," said the doctor. "I beg your pardon, my dear. It seems, in fact, that I'm in some trouble, here . . . owing to a little misunderstanding that I'll clear up in no time at all. Will you trust me to do that?"

She did not answer. She looked as white as Traynor felt. She loved this fellow . . . this murderer.

"In that case," said Channing, as though he had heard a long and bitter denunciation, "there's nothing to do but say good bye to you forever. May God bless you, Rose. I know you'll mix in a kind thought of me now and again."

He leaned, picked up the Stetson which Traynor had allowed to fall on the porch, and walked down the steps, down the path, out into the open street.

"Gentlemen," he said, lifting his hat to them, "what is it that you will have of me?"

III

Of course no eye that saw this picture could ever forget it. He stood out there in the sun with his hat raised, waiting, and running his eye up and down the waiting men of Little Snake, and not a voice answered, and not a hand was raised.

He turned his back, and walked without hurrying down the street, and around the corner. He was well out of view before a murmur grew out of the crowd. It increased to a loud humming. Then a yell broke out of one man. It was echoed by another. The whole crowd lurched suddenly into pursuit of Parker Channing, as fast as their feet would carry them.

"You look sick," said the cold voice of the girl to Traynor.

"I'm all right," he said.

He was not at all sure that he could walk, but he managed to get down the steps with sagging knees. When he stood on the level of the path, he turned to do his manners and lift his hat to Rose Laymon, but she was oblivious of him. She had her hands folded at the base of her throat. Her face was not contorted by sobbing, but tears of the exquisite agony of grief ran swiftly down her cheeks and splashed over her hands.

She loves him! said Traynor to himself. *She'll*

*never stop loving him. And . . . I wish to God that
I were dead!*

He got out from the grounds of the Laymon
house, at last, and turned into the emptiness
of that nice street. He had to take short steps.
His feet would not walk in a straight line, but
wandered a little crazily. Something akin to
nausea worked in his vitals. Something was dead
in him.

A pair of boys dashed on ponies around a
corner. When they saw him, they reined in their
horses. They swept about him in flashing arcs.
The hoofs of their ponies lifted a cloud of dust
that obscured Traynor.

"Yeller . . . yeller . . . yeller!" they shouted.
"Larry Traynor's yeller!"

They screamed and they sang the insult.

That was all right, and he might have done the
same thing at their age.

The thing was true. He was yellow. And yet
he still felt that it was the sick breathlessness
rather than actual terror that had kept his hands
idle back there on the verandah of the Laymon
house. All cowards, of course, would have the
same feeling. They were not afraid. No, no! They
were just troubled with a touch of ague. They felt
a mastering chill up the spine. They could not
help growing absent-minded because they were
thinking about home and mother.

He could have laughed. Instead, he had to start

34

gasping for air in real earnest. Something was profoundly wrong with him. And the two young devils kept wheeling their horses closer and closer to him, yelling more loudly. Other children were coming from the distance. Better to ask mercy from Indians than from these mannerless savages.

He saw the little house of the sheriff, unpainted, with nothing in what might have been a garden patch except the long hitching rack.

He turned in and climbed the verandah with weary legs.

"Look at him! He's afraid! Coward, coward, coward!" screamed the boy. "Oh, what a coward! He's yeller! Traynor is yeller!"

Traynor pushed the door open—it was never locked—and walked into the tiny, two-room house, kitchen-dining room—and then a small bedroom.

The sheriff had left in a hurry, this day, for the neatness of his housekeeping was marred by a soiled tin plate on the table, and a tin cup with coffee grounds still awash in the bottom of it.

Traynor went into the bedroom and lay down. The blankets held a heavy body odor that seemed to put away the supply of air.

He opened the front door and both windows. He opened the rear door to make a draft. Then he lay down on the floor of the kitchen and spread out his arms.

Lying on his back did no good. Presently he was sinking. A wavering thread attached him to existence, and the thread was running out, spinning thinner and thinner. To breathe very deeply took too much effort. He could only gasp in a profound breath every now and again when he was stifling.

He turned onto his right side, his head pillowed on his arm. By degrees he felt better.

He began to think of old Sam—dead. He began to ride again over the dusty miles the stagecoach had covered. Out of these thoughts he was recalled to himself by the sound of a horse trotting up to the front of the house, the squeak of saddle leather, the thump of feet as a man dismounted.

He sat up. Very strangely, the faintness had left him almost entirely. He rose to his feet, and a moment later the gray-headed sheriff walked into the room.

Compassion entered his eyes when he saw Traynor. Better to be hounded by the insults of the youngsters than to be met by that compassion. But the sheriff was a professional fighting man, and he was used to conduct of all kinds, no doubt.

He shook hands—almost too warily.

"Sit down, partner," he said. "I'm glad to see you. Mighty glad. I've heard about the stage . . . and everything. A good job you done in skinning away after that crook and getting his hat. We know who the killer is, now, and we'll have a chance to spot him one of those days. I hit the trail after him this evening."

He ran on cheerfully: "We've found out what made him do it. Faro. He couldn't keep away from the game, and Lem Samuels told us how much he was losing. You can't buy fine horses and trot a girl all around and then hit faro, too. So the poor fool found out about that shipment of cash and decided to help himself. A pretty cool nerve, Larry, when you come to think of it. A stagecoach filled with armed men and only one . . ."

Here the sheriff's voice died out, as though he realized that he was stepping on delicate ground.

"I'm mighty sorry about old Sam," he said. "One of the best men in the world . . . and a good friend to you, Larry. I hear the funeral is tomorrow morning."

"I won't be there," said Traynor. The sheriff waited, and he went on "I'll be pretty far out on a trail. And I want to carry handcuffs with me . . . and a deputy sheriff's badge."

The sheriff whistled softly. He laid his hand on the arm of Traynor.

"Ah, that's it, eh? Good boy, Larry. You were down for a minute, for the right sort of a fellow always comes back. If you want to go after the doctor, though, hadn't you better go with me?"

I'll go alone," said Traynor.

"Got an idea?"

"A piece of one."

"I'll swear you in," said the sheriff. "You know what you're doing. You shot his hat off, once . . . and I hope to God that you shoot his head off the next time . . . the damned, murdering, sneaking rat! Wait till I get a badge for you. . . ."

IV

The outfit that Traynor took was exactly what he wanted—some dry provisions, a pot and pan, a couple of blankets, a revolver and a rifle, enough ammunition. But his old horse, Tramper, was much too high to suit the rider. Tramper had not had much work to do since his master began to drive the stage. He had wandered through rich pasture lands, eating his fill, until his body was sleeked over with fat and his heart was rich with pride.

He wanted to dance every foot of the way; he insisted on shying at clouds, shadows, and old stumps, and in the morning he enjoyed working his kinks out with a little fancy bucking.

All of these things would have been nothing to the Traynor of the old days. He would have laughed at the dancing, the shying, the dancing, and pitching. But the Traynor who survived out of the past was a different fellow. A flurry of hard bucking left him gasping, head down, the landscape whirling before him. And it would be whole minutes before his breath came back to him. Even to sit the saddle for a few hours was a heavy thing, and he made it a habit to lie down flat beside the trail for a few minutes every couple of hours. Even so, he reached the end of each day almost exhausted.

But a good idea is better than strength to a determined man, and he had the idea.

Where would the doctor flee, when he rushed on his fine bay gelding out of Little Snake?

Of course he would wish to go far, but what was the greatest distance that he had ever gone from Little Snake through the twisting mountain trails?

A couple of months before, the doctor had been far up on Skunk Creek with a hunting party, and Skunk Creek was a good two days' ride away from the town. It seemed to Traynor a good bet that Channing would head for this distant place among the lonely mountains. From that point of vantage he could plan the rest of his retreat. The sheriff and his men would conscientiously hunt out the sign of the doctor's horse. Traynor preferred to hit far out and take his chance.

The second day was the worse of the two. The altitude made it harder for Traynor. He was continually short of breath. He was continually so very short that he had to gasp like a fish on dry land. About midday, also, he felt discomfort in his feet. By night they were so badly swollen about the ankles that he had to lie with his heels resting on a log higher than his head for a couple of hours before he could reduce the swelling and get his boots off.

In the morning of the third day he simply could not wedge his feet back into the boots. His feet were swelling out of shape. His wrists were heavy, also, and the cursed shortness of breath had increased.

But he was only an hour from the head of Skunk Creek, and he made that distance riding in his socks, his boots strapped on behind the saddle. Something had gotten into his system—some sort of poison, he presumed. And it was settling in his extremities. Some good, hard sweating when he got back into the heat of the valley would probably make all well.

Then he forgot his troubles of the body.

It was the glimmering verge of the day through which he rode. It was only the gray of the early dawn when he came down a gulley toward the head of Skunk Creek.

He thought, at first, that it was a wisp of morning mist that floated above the head of a cluster of aspens. But the mist kept rising, thin and small, always replenished.

It was fire smoke!

At the edge of the aspens he dismounted and leaned for an instant against the shoulder of the horse. His heart was rocketing in his body. His swollen feet were painful to stand on. His wrists were so thick that the rifle had a strange feeling in his grasp. His eyes felt heavy, too. He could

41

find pouches beneath them by the touch of his fingertips.

He looked for an instant about him. The rose of the morning had entered the gray dawn. The mountains shoved up black elbows against the brilliance of the sky.

It was his country, and he loved it. But the beauty of it gave him no joy, now. He could think of nothing except the horrible fluttering, the irregular pulsation of his heart, like a flock of birds beating their wings without a steady rhythm.

Was he to be mastered again—if indeed the smoke rose from the campfire of the doctor—not in battle but by the maudlin weakness of his own spirit?

Not spirit, either. Matters of the spirit do not puff the eyes or make the limbs swell.

Somewhere in the back of his mind he kept a sense of the old mountain tales of Indian witchcraft, and of evil spirits breathing into the bodies of condemned men by the ancient seers.

It was like that. That was how he felt exactly.

He went on gingerly through the copse.

Now, beyond the thinning of the trees, he could see the silhouette of a man saddling a horse. He drew closer. The veil of the trees thinned, and he found himself looking out on Dr. Parker Channing in person, in the act of drawing a bridle over the head of that lofty bay gelding. The gray flannel and the white shoes looked a good bit absurd in these mountain surroundings, however smart they had seemed in the town. But the air of the doctor had nothing absurd in it.

That lofty head was carried like a conqueror. The pair of holstered revolvers at the hips were not there for show, and the Winchester worn in a saddle holster would keep its owner fed fat with the best game the mountains could offer.

No matter what Channing had given up, he was not entirely depressed. It was the blue time of the day, of course, and yet he was singing a little to himself.

Something crackled behind Traynor. That idiot Tramper, of course, had followed where he was not wanted. He saw a shadowy impression of the horse behind him, and then the doctor was whirling with a drawn revolver.

"Hands up!" yelled Traynor.

"Damn the hands!" said Channing, and was firing into the trees at what must have been to him a very dim target.

Traynor, gun at shoulder, aimed at the breast and fired. He wanted it not this way but another way. Still he had to take the game as the doctor chose to play it.

He was certain, as he drew the trigger, that his forefinger was closing over the life of big Parker Channing. Then, as the rifle boomed, he heard the clang of the bullet against metal. The revolver, spinning out of the hands of the doctor, arched through the air, and struck heavily against the side of the gelding, which went off like a shot down the side of the creek. And out of the woods, squealing like a happy fool, Tramper bolted after this good example of light heels and a feather brain.

But Larry Traynor leaned a shoulder against a slender tree trunk and maintained his bead.

"Don't try for that second gun, Doctor," he said.

"Certainly not," said Channing politely. "But can it be my old friend . . . Traynor? Well met, my lad! Oh, if I'd only had one candlelight more of sunshine to show you to me among those trees!"

V

Fear ought not to choke a man when he has an enemy helpless under a levelled gun. Surely there was no fear in Traynor now, and yet his heart was still swelling in his throat, and his breath would not come as he walked out of the woods toward the doctor.

"Unbuckle that gun belt and drop it," he commanded.

Channing obeyed. His glance was not on the gun, but on the face of the captor.

"You're going fast, eh?" he asked.

"Going fast where?" demanded Traynor.

"To hell, old fellow," said the doctor.

And he kept shifting his glance across the face of Traynor as though he were reading large print.

"No, you won't last long," added Channing.

"Give me your hands," snapped Traynor.

"Here they are."

He held them out, and when he saw the handcuffs produced, he laughed.

"Ah, a legal arrest, eh? No murder, Larry? Just a legal arrest leading up to a trial, and all that?"

Traynor snapped the steel bracelets over the brown wrists of the other. And the doctor sneered openly.

"You poor devil. You can hardly breathe, can you?"

"Better than you'll be breathing before many days," said Traynor. "Step back, now."

The doctor stepped back. But he kept nodding and smiling, as though he were entirely pleased by what he saw. Traynor stooped and picked up the fallen gun belt. He strapped it around his own hips.

"I'm a little curious," said the doctor. "Have you been dealing with witches or good fairies, Larry? How could you manage to know that I'd come here?"

"You'd travel as far as you could over ground that you knew. This is the biggest march you ever made from Little Snake."

The doctor stared. "Well," he muttered, "I'll be damned. Am I as simple as all this? Then I deserve anything that comes to me."

He added, almost with a snarl: "I should have gone the entire way, on the Laymon verandah. I should have drifted some lead into you before the other people could see that you weren't able to fight. But . . . here we are, and what are you going to do?"

"Follow the infernal horses, first of all. Face that way, and march."

"How far, brother?" asked Channing, looking down at the feet of Traynor, which were softly muffled in socks.

"Till I wear the flesh off to the bone," Traynor said savagely.

"Is that it?" asked Channing. "I'm to be paraded through the streets of Little Snake with the conqueror behind me? Is that it?"

"Something like that," said Traynor. "You're going to parade into the Little Snake jail. I don't give a damn who sees you go."

"The fact is," said the doctor, rather with an air of curiosity than that of concern, "you never would have bothered about me, except that I seemed to have shamed you in front of your townsmen."

"The man you shot off the stage was my best friend," said Traynor. "You had to go down, Doctor, if I could manage to get a chance at you. I would have followed you the rest of my life."

"That wouldn't have been long, old son," chuckled Channing.

He looked again from the swollen feet to the puffed eyes of his captor. "No, that wouldn't have been long."

"Stop bearing down on me," commanded Traynor. "God knows that I am holding myself hard. I don't want to do you harm, Channing, but if you keep nagging me . . ."

They followed the two horses a good ten miles. Five of those miles were backtracking completely away from the direction of Little Snake, and at the end of that distance, from a hilltop Traynor bitterly watched the two animals careering miles and miles away from him down a gulch.

There was little use in following. He could not make Channing help him catch the horse that was to carry Channing to prison. And Traynor's feet were now in a condition that made walking difficult, running impossible.

Gloomily he turned in the direction of far-off Little Snake.

"March!" he said huskily.

The doctor laughed, and turned willingly in the appointed direction.

No man thinks of shoes until there is long marching to be done. But Traynor began to yearn for anything that would effectively clothe his feet. He had to cut off slabs of bark and bind them to his feet with strips of his clothes, which he sliced into bandages. Other bandages he used to wind around and around his ankles, and so constrict the swelling. But the puffiness which did not appear in the ankles began higher up the legs.

To walk began to be like wading through mud.

Yet through that entire day he kept heading on toward Little Snake.

In the evening he built a fire and stewed some rabbit, which he had shot along the way. They ate that meat. And the doctor sat with his back to the trunk of a tree and smoked cigarettes, and smiled pleasantly at his captor, in derision.

There was reason and plenty of it for that mockery, as Traynor knew. He had covered a truly short distance toward the town, and each day, it seemed, his feet were likely to grow worse and worse. If that were the case, before many days were out he would hardly be able to make perceptible headway.

Presently he said: "Channing, this is a thing to die of, eh?"

He pointed to his feet, to his wrists.

"Die? Why, you're dying now, man," Channing said. He laughed again. "You were dying down there in Little Snake, and I saw what was the matter with you when I looked at you on the verandah. Dying? You're as good as dead right now."

They were in the green bottom of a gulch, and the doctor looked around him with amused eyes.

"And yet," he said, "the medicine is here that will heal you. Make you fit and well again. Right here under your eyes, old man. I'll make the bargain with you. I'll take the swelling out of your legs and wrists . . . out of your whole dropsical body. And in exchange, I'm free to go where I please. What about that? What could be fairer than that?"

"I'll see you damned, first," answered Traynor softly.

Where could the healing stuff be? Traynor wondered. *In the bark of a tree? In roots of grass? In some mineral that the doctor had spotted in some small exposed vein?*

"Ignorance is the curse of you people," said Channing. "You ride your horses, raise your cattle, labor all your lives. Your amusements are drunkenness and gambling. Some of you marry and raise a batch of equally damned children to follow your own dark ways. In the end, men of intelligence come, exploit the opportunities that you have opened to them, and elbow you out of your holdings. And that is fit and right, Traynor. In the eye of superior beings like myself, you and your friend on the driver's seat were no more than wild hogs running loose in the forest."

Traynor gripped his rifle with an instinctive gesture.

He laid the gun back as suddenly.

"No," he said. "That would be the easiest way for you, Channing. Dying wouldn't bother you. But to be shamed in front of a lot of people . . . to have Rose pitying you and despising you . . . that would be the real hell . . . and, by God, you're going to taste plenty of it before I'm through."

He felt very faint, so he tied the doctor to a tree before he lay down for the night. Afterward, he slept brokenly and in the earliest dawn he resumed the march.

Not for Little Snake. He knew, now, that he

could never make the town. There was a much nearer goal. By swinging to the south, he would reach the next outlying ranch—the Laymon place, thirty good miles from Little Snake. Once there, his prisoner would be safely in the hands of the law, old John Laymon, that fiercest of all the enemies of evil-doers, would see to it that Channing was handed over to the sheriff. And the sheriff would see to it that Parker Channing was hanged by the neck till he was dead!

So to the south they marched that day. At noon, Traynor told himself that he would go no farther, his ankles and wrists had become elephantine. His eyes were puffed until his vision was dim, and inside his breast there was continually that cursed beating as of wings, great and small, in hurried and irregular flight.

If he lay down on his left side, during one of the many rest periods, it seemed to him that he was slipping down, being moved feet first—for the sound of his heart was like the rubbing of two bodies together—like the vibration of a wet finger against a pane of glass.

There was constant pain. There was constant faintness.

That night, the huge watery puffing of his flesh suggested something that might ease him. He cut shallow gashes with his knife. Not blood but water flowed out, in quantity. That was a relief,

51

and when the morning came neither wrists nor ankles seemed to have regained their swollen proportions of the evening before.

Every night, thereafter, he made new incisions or freshened the old ones so that the water would run out of his flesh. In the middle of the next day's march, the cuts would begin to bleed—blood and water commingled.

His eyes were growing bad, very bad. It was difficult for him to shoot game. Images wavered before him. But on the third day chance enabled him to shoot a deer. Afterward, he could load the prisoner with venison and make him carry the food for the party.

"The worst diet in the world for you, Larry," the doctor said cheerfully. "You're dying, anyway, but you'll die all the sooner under the effect of this diet. Do you want to know how really bad you are? Cut a reed there on the bank of the creek. Put one end to your ear and the other end to your heart. It will be a sort of stethoscope, old son. You can study your death more clearly, that way."

Traynor cut out the reed. He was able to bend without breaking it, and with one end to his ear and the other pressed to his breast, he listened to the queer, hurrying, faint vibration of the heart. It passed into flurries so mild and dim that he could not begin to count the contractions. It seemed to him that legions of ghosts were flickering across his vision. And again there were breathless, frightful pauses in which he was sure the next stroke would never come, and at the end of those pauses would come one hellish, bell-like stroke that sent a thin shudder all through his being.

He looked up at the sneering, smiling face of the doctor.

"Say, Parker," he said, "I'm a dying man, right enough."

"But why die, fool?" asked Channing lightly. "Life all around you! Life . . . life . . . life!"

And he began to laugh, blowing out his cigarette smoke in ragged clouds of mirth.

"Presently you're going to fall into a coma. That will be the end, my dear Larry."

"It's true," Larry Traynor said. "I'm going to pass out. You'll brain me with the handcuffs while I'm helpless. And that's why . . . that's why, after all, I have to do this."

"Do what?" Channing asked cheerfully.

To stand entailed too great an effort. That was why Larry Traynor only pushed himself up to one knee. He raised the rifle and levelled it.

"You have to die, Channing," he said. "I won't be far behind you, I suppose . . . but you'll have to go before me."

"Right," said the doctor. "Either way . . . it makes little difference to me. But what a fool bulldog you are! Blind, stupid, with fat in your brain!"

Down the barrel of the gun, Traynor sighted. He covered the breast. He covered the face. He drew his bead between the bright eyes. Just where the bullet had knocked the life out of the buckskin leader.

VI

There was no doubt that Parker Channing, the doctor, was a brave man, a very brave man. He sat steady enough. He held up his head high. But to look at death is not an easy thing, and, as the seconds ran on, the eyes of Channing began to enlarge and grow too bright.

Suddenly he shouted: "Shoot, damn you!"

Traynor lowered the gun. "I've been trying to. I've been wanting to," he said slowly. "But I can't. I don't suppose I have the nerve to shoot even a . . . dog!"

He cast the rifle from him and sat with his head between his hands.

"The poorest fool," laughed the doctor, "the weakest and the poorest fool that I've ever met!"

There was a ridge between them and the valley in which the house of Laymon stood. They climbed that ridge.

It was only a few miles to go, but it took them four days. Sometimes the dying man walked. Sometimes he crawled.

He would hear the doctor say: "Keep your drooling mouth shut, will you?"

And then he would realize that he had been walking with his mouth open, babbling meaningless words.

For the agony had ground out his brain. His wits were spinning. And death was carried inside him, in his very heart.

It was on the second day of moiling and toiling up that slope that he reached a little pool of still water and looked at his face in the mirror. The thing he saw turned him sick. It could not be him. But when he opened his mouth, the bloated lips of the image opened, also.

That day, the doctor said: "To do a thing like this for the sake of fame . . . aye, there's sense in that. But to do it for nothing . . . to do it for the sake of a little hand-clapping in a village filled with muddy-brained yokels . . . by God, Traynor, I've never heard of such insanity. I'm going to take back some of the other things I've said to you. Whatever else you are, as a bulldog, you're magnificent. You're killing yourself for a crazy sense of justice. What good will the legal murder of me do to the soul of your dead friend? And if you'll make the bargain with me, I'll have you practically fit and well inside of three days. Will you listen to me?"

Traynor did not answer. He was saving his breath because he seemed to need it all. The deadly tremor was entering him more deeply than ever.

They got over the ridge the next day. Below them, Traynor could see sprawling lines of the ranch house and the barns, and the shining tangle of the barbed-wire fencing of the corrals.

That was the goal, under his eyes, in his hand. It was not three miles away.

It took them five days to cover the three miles, though nearly every step of the way was downhill.

But the point was that he took not so many steps. He was on his knees, waddling, most of the time. The knees grew bruised. But mere pain was nothing—nothing at all. The burning of the gashes in his legs helped to keep his wits awake.

He had cut away most of his clothes for bandages, by this time. More than half naked, blood-stained, swollen to a frightful grossness, he could not look down on his body without loathing.

The fourth evening found him still a full mile from the goal. He sat back against a tree, half blind, covering his prisoner constantly with the rifle, though he could only get the tip of a swollen finger inside the trigger guard. And lying there, with an aching throat and a groaning voice, he prayed aloud to God.

He fired shot after shot. He fired them in groups of three, sure signals for help. And yet not a single rider rushed out from the ranch to help him. For four days he had been close enough to catch the attention of some range rider. But when he fired the gun, there was no response—there was only the mocking laughter of the doctor.

But for the fifth day he mustered the last of his strength and the whole exhaustless mass of his courage to bridge the final gap. And it was bridged. Just as the sunset was nearing, that poor, rolling monster and his handcuffed man reached the back door of the ranch house. The steps up to the porch seemed to Traynor almost as insurmountable as any alp.

He shouted, and he had no answer except a feeble echo that flew back to him from the bald, vacant faces of the barns.

Then Channing said: "I've saved something to tell you. I'll tell it to you now. And be damned to you. I've been crowing over you these five days because, you fool, the ranch is empty! There's nobody in the house. All these five days your bleary eyes couldn't make out the details, but I've seen that not a single soul has left this house or entered it."

"It can't be empty. It's the Laymon place," mumbled Traynor. "You've got to be wrong. You've got to be lying. It's the great Laymon place . . . and . . ."

"If you had something besides death and cotton-batting in your brain," shouted the doctor, "you would have noticed that there are no cattle in the fields! Not a damned one. The place has been cleaned up!"

Traynor waited for a moment. He could see

very little. Off toward the west there was a redness in the sky, to be sure. Red . . . fire . . . and fire . . . as in his wounds, and ghastly fogs of death were in his brain.

This was the end of the trail, at last.

He said: "Doctor, you ought to die. I wanted to see you hanged."

"Thanks, old son," said Channing. "I've been appreciating that idea of yours for some days, you know."

"I could chain you here in the house . . . if it's empty . . . and you'd starve in three days."

The doctor said nothing.

"That wouldn't be pretty, eh? You tied and starving . . . and me spilled out on the floor, my body rotting away as I die. Not pretty, Doctor, eh?"

"My God, no," breathed the doctor.

"Well," said Traynor, "I can't do it. I'll tell you why. I can't help remembering that Rose loved you. I can't do you in like this, Channing."

He had to pause and fight for breath.

The captive stared at him with eyes made enormous by wonder.

"Inside this right hand trousers pocket," said Traynor. "There's the key to the handcuffs, there. You take it . . . I can't get my hand into the pocket anymore. Take it, and set yourself free." He laid down his gun as he spoke.

The doctor, his hands trembling so that the

chain between the handcuffs sang a tuneless song, reached into the pocket, found the key.

When he had it, he stood over his captor for a moment with his hands raised as though he intended to dash the steel manacles into the hideously distorted face.

VII

Pain in Traynor had reached such a point that he could not fear death itself. That was why he waited for the blow with a frightful caricature of a smile. He felt that this was natural.

He had given the tiger its freedom, and the first place the tiger struck would be at him.

But Parker Channing stood back, after a moment. He scowled at Traynor. He fitted the key into the lock of the handcuffs, and in an instant he was free. A wild, strange cry burst from his throat. He hurled the manacles far away from him, and his glance wandered across the mountains—freedom and safety lay for him there. The discarded hope of existence returned to him with a rush. Joy blossomed like a flower in his face.

From that prospect, he looked back suddenly at the helpless man who lay against the steps of the verandah. The sight made him sneer. He moved as though he would spurn at the shapeless face. As for the bloated, visionless eyes, there was little comprehension in them. To crush Traynor, now, would be like crushing a foul toad.

But something else was working in the mind of the doctor. It made him take a few paces up and down, muttering to himself. He wanted to be away. He wanted to be putting miles of safety between himself and the society which had no more use for him now than to strangle him at the end of a rope.

And still the dim life in the eyes of Traynor held him back.

He uttered a final exclamation and stepped away.

Traynor looked after him without denunciation, without hope. Even thinking had grown to be a frightful effort. It was better to lie back and feel the damp cold of the night coming over him. It was better to lie still with the dreadful fluttering in his breast, the movement as of dying wings, wings that have flown to weariness over a sea of darkness into which they must fall.

It would not be long now. Very shortly, as the night closed over him, his eyes would be closed and never open.

A returning footfall amazed him. Through the dimness he saw the tall form of the doctor go past him, up the slope, across the verandah. A little pause at the door, and Channing entered the house. His footfall echoed through the emptiness. There was the rattling of iron, sounding iron like that of a stave. Finally the dying man heard the crackling of a fire, more cheerful than the song of a cricket. Pans rattled. A fragrance of cookery moved out on the night air.

The doctor was low, very low, but even in him

it was a peculiar monstrosity that he should cook for his own comfort while a man lay dying within sense range of the preparation of the food.

The footfall came loudly out of the kitchen, across the verandah, and descended.

"Stand up!" commanded the harsh voice of the doctor.

"No use," said Traynor. "If I'm in your way here, roll me out of the path. I'm not moving anymore."

"Look," said Channing. "You're like a rotten bit of flesh. You're rotten all through. I don't want to touch you. But . . . if you'll try to get up, I'll do something for you."

"Thanks," said Traynor. "And . . . to hell with you, Channing."

The doctor sighed. He leaned. He fitted his strong hands under the shoulders of Traynor and raised him to a sitting posture.

The brain of Traynor whirled dizzily.

"Let me be," he said in a husky whisper. "I'm almost finished, Channing. Let me pass out, this way . . . no more pain . . . God! . . . let it finish off like this . . . downhill. . . ."

The fierce hands of the doctor, strong, hard, painful, ground into his flesh and raised him. He was tottering on his feet. Now he went forward, his huge, hippopotamus feet bumping together as he was more than half lifted up the steps.

The kitchen stove, as they entered the room, he

heard roaring with fire. A lamp had been lighted. Wisps of smoke were twisting in the air above the stove, and pans over the fire were trembling a little with the force of the flames. Dim hope, now, entered the mind of Traynor. For fire is the servant of man, and works miracles for him.

The doctor got him down the hall and turned him through a doorway into another lighted room. On the incredible softness of a bed he stretched the body of Traynor. He covered him with blankets.

"Stop thinking," said the doctor, standing over his patient. "Don't do any more thinking. It'll wear out your mind. Look at the light. Remember that you're not going to die."

"Not die?" whispered Traynor.

"No."

"Not die?" murmured Traynor again, and his mouth remained gaping open, as though he were drinking in hope with the air.

The doctor left. He returned, after a little, with a cup of tea. He raised the bloated, spongy head of Traynor in the crook of his arm. The tea had a foul odor. The taste of it was green, bitter, sick.

"Pretty bad to swallow, eh?" asked Channing. "But it's life, Traynor. This is the life that was green all around you, as we came through the valleys. Foxglove, Traynor. It's the plant that doctors get digitalis from. Do you know why your body is almost rotting away from you? It's because your heart has gone bad. And digitalis is going to cure that heart. When your heart is well, you'll be well . . . you'll be well. You'll be fit for a normal life again. Here . . . finish this stuff off and then I'll make some more."

And Traynor drank the foul stuff and almost found it good, it was so sweetened by the taste of hope!

In twenty-four hours, the change was incredible. The bloating about the face was almost entirely gone. The whole body and the limbs of Traynor felt lighter. Above all, he could see clearly, he could think clearly, and as he stared up at the ceiling, his thoughts led him into a continual maze of wonder.

Channing came back into the room that evening with food, and more of the digitalis tea. Now that the brain and the eyes of Traynor were clearer, he could catch in the face of the doctor the shadow of distaste as he looked down upon the sick man, but mastering that dislike, that horror, there was a keen interest showing through.

He fed Traynor. He held the cup of tea for him, raising his head.

Afterward, he pulled the soggy clothes from the body of Traynor and washed the sick man. The exquisite comfort of cleanliness soaked through the flesh, into the soul of Traynor. He had felt too dirty to be worth life.

Yet, from day to day, the strength flowed back into his body, into his brain. And the frightful fluttering of wings had left his breast. When he turned on his left side, he could still feel a slight, quick, abnormal vibration, but, otherwise, the beating of the heart did not trouble him except that now and then there would be a great, single drum stroke, as though to give him warning of the condition in which he had once lain.

"The digitalis . . . it's done all this?" he asked, marveling.

"I'll tell you how it came to be discovered," said Channing. "There was an old woman in England who used to cure people with dropsy by giving them a tea. There were twenty or thirty herbs in that tea. And it certainly worked . . . on that sort of dropsy that comes from heart trouble. So a doctor with a brain able to ask a question and try to answer it, took specimens of that tea, made the same brew, and then eliminated one of the herbs after the other. When the digitalis was left in, the tea still worked . . . it was good for people with bad hearts. When the digitalis was left out, the tea was no good at all, except to leave a bad taste in the mouth. That was how the drug was discovered. It is one of the few that are absolutely necessary to doctors today. It works miracles. You're one of the miracles. You look like a human being again . . . you *are* a human being. You're able to sit up. You could start walking tomorrow . . . and that's the day I leave you, Traynor."

Traynor stared upward at the ceiling.

"Why did you do this, Parker?" he asked.

"I don't know," answered Channing, scowling. "Partly because you were such a bulldog. Partly because . . . well, because the doctor in me was being tormented by the sight of you. My profession is sworn to relieve suffering, you know."

"You know how you'll be repaid for making me well?"

"I don't know."

"As soon as I can walk and ride, I'm coming on your trail again."

"Good!" exclaimed Parker Channing. "No damned sentimentality. And we'll fight out the good cause to a finish."

"We will," said Traynor.

He smiled in a strange way at Channing, and Channing smiled in the same manner back at his patient.

"I understand," said Traynor.

"What do you understand?"

"Why it'll be a pleasure to you to cut my throat . . . it's because you can't stand the idea of my finding Rose Laymon again, and making her forget that the crooked doctor ever lived."

"You'll never make her forget me," Channing said, scowling.

"Women know how to put things out of their minds," insisted Traynor.

"Let's talk no more about it!" he exclaimed, and straightaway left the room.

Their understanding was perfect, Traynor knew. They had made a fair exchange. To the doctor he had restored freedom, and the doctor had given him health and life. Neither needed to be grateful to the other. It was a fair exchange and they could part equal. Yet, except for the picture of old Sam lying on his back in the dust of the road—except for that still vivid image, Traynor knew that he could be fond of this man.

He was simply an outcross from the ordinary blood of humanity.

His brain worked not as the brains of other men. There was a greater logic in him, a coldness of brain. When he was in need of money, he was able to conceive a crime. Having conceived the crime, he was able to execute it calmly, efficiently, killing the old hero who attempted to interfere with his scheme.

This picture of cold-minded efficiency was marred by only two facts—the real love of the doctor for Rose Laymon, and the weakness of mind which forced him to tend his worst enemy, curing a patient who would afterward go on the trail to end his life if possible.

These thoughts were in the mind of Traynor

68

that evening. In the morning, the doctor would go, sinking himself deep into the mountains, securing his freedom from pursuit. And Traynor would wait one day, recovering further strength before he started the long walk back to Little Snake.

He could hear the pounding hoofs of a horse up the road; the doctor was stirring about in the kitchen, singing softly.

The noise of the horse turned in toward the ranch house.

Hinges creaked with a great groaning and vibration, as though a wooden gate were being dragged open. After that, the sounds of the horse came closer.

The doctor was no longer moving in the kitchen.

His step came down the hall. He looked in at the door of his sick man. There was a rifle in his hands.

"Somebody's coming. I guess this is good bye, Larry," he said.

"Good luck . . . till I meet you again," said Traynor.

"Aye," sneered the doctor. "The same to you . . . till I sink lead into you. . . ."

The noise of the horse had ended. A footfall sounded on the back porch as the doctor turned to slip away through the front of the house.

He was checked by a voice that rang clearly

through the old building, calling: "Hello! Who's there? Who's here?"

Channing whirled about as though a knife had dug into him. For that was the unforgettable voice of Rose Laymon.

VIII

The doctor leaned the rifle against the wall. He looked white, strained, old.

"Call her," he whispered to Traynor.

"All right." He lifted his voice. "Rose! I'm in here!"

And the girl answered: "Who . . . Larry Traynor?"

She came running. At the door of the room she halted. Her riding had blown color into her face. The hat was well back on her head. And there was such an upwelling of light in her eyes, such a gleaming of surprise and caution and excitement, that she looked to Traynor more beautiful than ever.

"Larry," she exclaimed, "are you ill? What's the matter? Did you catch up with him? Did that murderer hurt you . . . ?"

She was coming into the room, a small step at a time, when she saw the doctor in the corner, among the shadows, she winced from him with a guttural exclamation, as though she had been struck.

The doctor, whiter than ever, made a small gesture.

"Murderer is the word, Rose . . . but not a woman-killer, you know."

She faced the doctor, but she kept backing up until she was close to the bedside of Larry Traynor. There she put out a small hand, and Traynor took it. He could see an agony in the face of Channing at this gesture which sprang from fear of him.

Then the doctor mastered himself. He spoke almost lightly. "Why not sit down, Rose?" he asked. "I was leaving in the morning . . . but I'll get out tonight since you've arrived. However, we might all have a chat together."

Her hand wandered behind her, found a chair, drew it toward her while her eyes were still fixed on the doctor. She sat down, close to Larry Traynor.

It seemed as though she had stepped far back in time to the last moment when they had meant so much to one another. With a gesture, in an instant, she had banished the distance that had come between them.

And Traynor, turning his own head away from the doctor, watched the breathing of the girl, and his soul extended toward her with an immensity of joy and possession.

"I don't understand it," she said, shaking her head. "Will you tell me what's happened, Parker . . . that you seem to be here with Larry . . . like a friend?"

"He caught me, and slipped the handcuffs on me," said the doctor. He brought out his words with a cool precision. "His heart went bad on the march in. He turned off to this place to shorten the way. He was close to dying when he got here . . . and instead of sending me to hell before him, he turned me loose, so I cured his heart trouble for him. We part tomorrow. And we'll meet another day on another trail."

His glance collected an intensity of hatred as he stared at Traynor.

Yet he went on, forcing himself: "When you and the fools of Little Snake thought that he was showing the white feather, the other day . . . that was simply the same heart trouble. I saw the tremble and jump of the pulse in his throat, and I knew that he was as helpless as a child."

The effort of that full statement of the facts left the doctor panting.

He said to Traynor: "I think this leaves us quits, Larry."

"Absolutely quits," agreed Traynor.

She almost turned her back on the doctor as she leaned over Traynor.

"You know what I thought that day, Larry?" she said. "Yes, because you could see it in my face. Are you going to forgive me?"

"Look," said Traynor. "That didn't happen . . . that's forgotten. The other things . . . what's to come . . . that's all that matters."

A slight shadow—like fear—ran across her eyes as he had many times seen a cloud-shadow run across the bright green of a spring landscape. But then she smiled at him. There was that in her smile that made him glad not to look toward the doctor.

"I'll be getting on," said Channing.

"You can't go," she said. "Not till I've thanked you for the thing you've done for Larry."

The face of Channing withered with pain.

"That's unnecessary cruelty, isn't it?" he asked.

"Parker, be honest," she said. "It was all a game with you. You never cared a whit about me. I was simply a girl to fill some of the dull hours, isn't that the truth?"

He stared at her.

"All right," he said. "We'd better let it rest that way." Then he added: "No decent girl wants to think that a murderer ever cared for her."

"You're being serious?" she asked.

"My God," he said, "even if there's no heart in you, there ought to be a memory."

"There is a memory," she answered. "You meant everything? Did you really mean everything, Parker?"

"There's no good in talking about it," Channing said. "I know what I'm going to do. I've seen what you think of me now. But so far as meaning what I've said before . . . well, I meant more than that even when the damned supercilious air I was born with was denying my words."

After this, there was a pause that alarmed

Traynor. He began to look anxiously from one to the other. And when he saw her beauty and the magnificence of the doctor, he could not help feeling that in some way they had been made and destined for one another.

Then she said: "I'm sorry, Parker."

"You mean that," he answered very slowly. "And I'm such a poor beggar now that I'm grateful even for pity. Or is your blood still running cold when you look at me?"

"No," she said, shaking her head. "Only it's the horrible waste, Parker. It's the frightful throwing away of all your chances . . . it's the ending of your life that makes me want to cry."

"That's maudlin sentimentality," he answered, half sneering. "I'm ashamed of you, Rose. That's the weak streak appearing. As a matter of fact, I'll find my way to a new place in the world. Our friend Traynor thinks that he'll be able to find me on the out trail and stop me. For his own sake, I hope that he doesn't reach me . . . ever."

And once more there was murder in the glance he gave Traynor. And a sort of hunger came up in the heart of Larry Traynor for that future day when he would be able to confront the doctor clad in his full strength, without that deadly betrayal, that horrible fluttering of the heart and the nerves.

"I'll go now," said Channing.

"You can't go," said the girl. "You can't leave me alone with Larry. And I won't leave him here in danger."

"Danger?" echoed the doctor.

"Of course. The Whartons may swoop on the place at any time. And they . . ."

"The Whartons are in prison!" exclaimed Channing.

"They *were* in prison . . . haven't you seen a newspaper? They broke jail. They, and a dozen other men. They started away through the mountains. They've been sighted here and there, getting closer and closer to this place."

"Ah," said the doctor, "and that's why your father moved off the place . . . with the cattle and all?"

"That's right. The instant he knew that the Whartons were free, he was sure that they'd come as fast as they could straight for the ranch. He knew that they'd run off the cattle and burn the buildings. So he started straight for town."

"Why couldn't he have brought out a posse from town?"

"Hire thirty men for heaven knows how long? At five dollars a day and keep? He would rather die than throw away money like that."

The doctor nodded.

"Rose," said Traynor, "do you mean that the Whartons may come down on this place at any moment?"

"It's true. They were sighted two days ago in Tomlinson's gulch."

"Then what under heaven made you come out here . . . at night . . . into the danger?"

"I'm ashamed to tell you why I came," said the girl, blushing. "Well, I don't care . . . I'll show you!"

She ran from the room. Her footfall went lightly down the hall, and Traynor smiled, listening after it, until his absent-minded glance crossed the burning eye of the doctor.

"Some way . . . ," said the doctor.

He did not need to complete that tight-lipped sentence.

"Some way" he would manage to cross and blast the happiness which was dawning again for Larry Traynor.

The cold white devil in his face glared steadily out at Traynor.

The girl came back. In her hands she held up a rose-colored frock, covered with airy flounces, the square-cut neck bordered with a film of lace.

"My first party dress," she said. "I looked through the luggage that father brought in . . . When I couldn't find it, I made up my mind that I'd take this trip. I wouldn't risk the lives of men by asking them to come along. So, I told mother that I was going to spend the night with Martha Carey . . . and then I came out here. I could be back long before the morning."

No matter what enmity was between them, the two men looked at one another and smiled.

Rose, lowering the dress, suddenly cried out in a stifled voice of fear.

Traynor followed the glance, and at the window, pressed so close to the pane that the nose and chin were whitened, he saw a man's face, rounded out like an owl's with an uncropped growth of beard, a man with eyes narrowed in the most hellish malice. And the upper lip curled back from the teeth as though the man were a carnivorous creature, a hunting beast of the night.

The face receded, sank out of sight like a stone wavering down into the dark depths of a pool.

"It's Jim Wharton!" gasped the girl. She slid down on her knees. "Oh, God, it's Jim . . . and all the rest will be with him!"

IX

The doctor got to thinking with a leap, catching up the rifle on the way. He pulled up the sash and thrust the rifle out.

A bullet smashed through the glass, thudded into the opposite wall, and the doctor stepped back into the corner, while still loosened bits of the glass were falling with a tinkle to the floor.

Traynor, half undressed under the blankets, threw back the covers and began to pull on the rest of his clothes. He had shaped some heavy felt moccasins which he stepped into now.

"I've got to get Larry out!" Rose was crying. "He can't take care of himself, now. Parker, we've got to get Larry out."

"Do we?" Channing asked calmly. "We'll be in luck if we get anyone out."

He walked from the room and down the hall. Traynor followed. He was weak in the knees, and his head was light, but the gashes in his legs were fairly healed. He would have strength for short efforts, he felt sure.

They stood in the kitchen. The lamp had burned low and crookedly. It was smoking fast, and the sickening sweet smell of the soot hung in the air.

The doctor took control.

"I'm going to try the back door, quietly," he said. "It may be that they haven't scattered all around the house, yet. If I get out, you two sneak after me. Keep on the left. We'll try to get to the shrubs. . . ."

Traynor had neared the door. It was perfectly apparent to him that the doctor was willing to take the risks. But there was a good reason why he should not.

Through the screen on the door, Traynor could see the pale glimmer of the moonlight. It was thin. It poured like a haze of brilliance over the ground. He could see the gleam of strands of new wire along the corral fence. The barns were half white, half black shadow. The scene had the very look of death.

The doctor was still speaking when Traynor pushed the door soundlessly open and stepped out onto the porch. He had not taken two steps when he heard the stifled exclamation of Rose Laymon behind him.

The doctor muttered: "Come back, you fool. . . ."

Then, out of the cloudy dark of a bank of shrubs behind the house, a thin tongue of flame darted, disappeared. The crack of the rifle struck painfully against his ears. A sting greater than that of a giant hornet gashed Traynor's neck.

He jerked the door open and stood back in the kitchen. A bullet hissed beside his ear as he side-stepped.

"They're behind the house . . . they're all around the house, it seems," said Traynor.

The girl parted her lips to speak, but no words came. She stood in white suspense while the doctor grabbed Traynor by the shoulders.

"You jack-ass," snarled Channing, examining the wound on Traynor's neck. "This thing . . . thank God it's only a scratch."

He pulled out a handkerchief and began to bind up the neck of Traynor.

"Why did you do it, Larry?" begged the girl. "Why, why did you go out there . . . help- . . . helpless. . . ."

"It's the glory that the fool wants! Glory!" sneered the doctor.

"Mind you," said Traynor, "I'll be no good to the rest of you. They're going to get me before the show's over, and they might as well get me now. You're the fool, Parker. You're the able-bodied man. It's up to you to get Rose away. You can't show yourself here and there to draw fire."

Channing, finishing the bandaging, stepped suddenly back at the end of this speech. The girl, with moisture welling into her eyes, stared mutely at Traynor.

"You see what he is," sneered the doctor. "A hero, eh? A dead hero before long, I suppose."

"We're all dead, Rose," Traynor said. "And this is no time for damned heroics or . . . ," he stopped suddenly. He put his hand up, commanding: "Listen!"

Outside, a man shouted. He was answered far

and near, from all around the house, by what seemed a score of voices.

"We're walled in," said the doctor.

Traynor sat down and leaned his elbows on the edge of the table. He looked at the floor, forcing his eyes down because he did not want to let the image of Rose fill them. He tried to bend his mind away from the thought of her. As for what happened to him and the doctor, it was no tragedy. Men who live with guns in their hands have to fall by guns in the end, often enough. They were simply playing out their logical parts. But the girl—she stood beside him, now resting a hand on his shoulder.

The doctor paced the floor like a great cat.

No one spoke. The nearness of the danger blinded their eyes and stopped thought.

Then a voice called: "Hello, you inside, there!"

The doctor placed himself close to the door.

"Hello, outside," he answered.

"Who are you?"

"I'm Doctor Parker Channing."

"You're Doctor Murderer Channing, are you?"

"I'm the man."

Sneering, drawling laughter commented on his name and presence.

"Channing, you'd be better outside than inside. We could use a doctor like you."

"I suppose you could," said Channing,

"Open that door and walk out to our side of

the fence, and you'll be as safe as any of us."

Channing looked down at his hands and dusted them.

"Go on, Parker," urged the girl. "It's the best thing for you. You'll be safer with them than anywhere else. With them you may have a chance to get away. . . ."

"What do you suggest, Larry?" asked the hard voice of the doctor.

"You're a fool if you don't go out to them," said Traynor, peering into the pale face of Channing. "But I think you're going to be a fool."

"Do you?" asked the doctor, with a slight start. "Thanks!"

"Answer up, Doc!" shouted the man outside.

"Who are you?" called Channing.

"I'm Jim Wharton."

"Wharton, I'm staying in the house with my friends."

A yell of amazement answered him.

"Are you crazy, Channing? Are you gonna go home with your friends and let the sheriff hang you?"

"I'm staying here. That's final."

"Of all the damned fools!" thundered Wharton.

He added, a moment later: "There's another offer I'll make to you."

"Let's hear it!" called the doctor.

"Who's the second man in there . . . the one that was flat in bed?"

"That's Larry Traynor."

"Traynor? I got nothing against him. Now, listen to me."

"I'm listening."

"I've got men all around the house."

"I know that."

"Then you know that we can do what we please."

"I know that, too. But it might cost you something."

"Damn the cost. Or else, I can burn you out. And that's what I'll do if I have to!"

The doctor said nothing. But his head bowed a little and he took a great breath. Men whose nerve is equal to all other things are often horrified and unmanned by the thought of fire.

"But there's an easy way out of all this," went on Jim Wharton. "It ain't everybody in the world that I'm against. It's that skunk that put me in jail. It's John Laymon that I'm going to get even with. Send out the girl to me. She's in there. I seen her myself."

"What sort of a hound do you think I am?" asked the doctor.

"I think you got brains. I hope you have, anyway. We won't touch her. But we'll hold her till her old man pays to get her back . . . and pays heavy. Damn him, he's got enough money to pay. And I'm going to have a slice of it . . . a slice right into the red of it!"

The doctor turned his head from the door toward Traynor and Rose Laymon. His eyes were glazed.

Traynor, starting to speak, found the hand of the girl over his mouth.

The doctor seemed to see nothing.

"Answer up!" yelled Jim Wharton. "If you think that I'm going to wait an hour, you're nutty. I get the girl, or else I burn out the three of you, like rats."

Suddenly the girl cried out sharply: "I'll come to you, Jim!"

"Good girl!" yelled Wharton. "You'll be safe with us, Rose."

She had started up. The grip of Traynor fell on her wrist and checked her.

"Let me go, Larry!" she panted. "There's no other way for the two of you . . ."

"They won't harm her," said the doctor. "They won't hurt her. She'll be safe, Larry, and . . . and . . ."

His voice faded. The last words he merely gibbered. The high pride from the doctor had weakened and melted away so close to the fierce face of danger.

"What he says is true!" cried Rose Laymon. "Larry, don't you see that . . ."

"Be still!" said Traynor sternly. He jerked her down into a chair at his side. Then, his grim eyes never leaving the face of the doctor, he said:

"You'd trust her with a gang of dogs like those fellows outside?"

"She'd be all right," panted the doctor. "She'd be . . . I mean . . . fire, Larry. My God, if they set fire to any of these wooden building . . . the flames would run faster than horses . . . they'd . . . God . . . they'd see us. . . ."

"Are you coming, Rose?" shouted Jim Wharton.

"Be still!" ordered Traynor.

"You damned fool!" shrieked the doctor, his voice shaking to pieces on the high note, "do you want her to be burned to death?"

"Aye, better that than the other thing," said Traynor. "Channing, what a dog you are, after all."

"Rose! Rose!" called Wharton. "Where are you?"

And a great voice came out of her throat as she answered: "I'm not coming, Jim. I'm staying here!"

"Rose, if you stay there . . . woman or no woman . . . I'll fire the house. Do you hear what I'm telling you?"

"I hear . . . and I'm staying. . . ."

"That's crazy!" panted the doctor. "It's . . . fire, Rose . . . they'll burn the house over our heads. They'll . . ."

"Go out and argue with them," said Traynor sternly. "Maybe you can make them change their minds."

Parker Channing, leaning against the wall, struck a fist into his wan face and groaned.

Then he muttered: "I'll talk to them . . . face to face . . . I'm not afraid. . . ."

"I've given you your last chance!" yelled Jim Wharton. "Of all the damned . . ."

"Wait a minute!" screamed the doctor. "I'm coming out . . . I'm coming out to talk to you . . . I'm going to . . ."

He opened the door.

"Can I come . . . safely?" he shouted again.

"Aye, come ahead."

And Dr. Parker Channing slunk out of the house, without a word to those who remained behind.

They knew that he would not come back.

The screen door slammed, rebounded with a jingle, slammed again.

"He's gone," whispered Rose Laymon. "Oh, Larry . . . for him to go . . . murder was nothing compared to this."

A queer pain wrung the soul of Larry Traynor.

"He's a brave man, though. I've seen him laugh at the idea of dying. Aye, with a gun levelled at him. But the fire, Rose . . . that's the thought that killed the heart in him. Never name him again. The life that's in me, it's Parker that gave it back to me. He wouldn't be here now, except that he stayed to take care of me."

And a voice rolled in on them, faint from distance: "Throw the brush up there against the side of the house. Light that straw and throw it on, too."

X

They could tell the course of the fire by the rising yells of the Wharton gang and then the noise of the flames was perceptible, and finally a tremor that went through the whole building. Beyond the window, they saw the smoke driving low in the wind toward the barns, which were wrapped in clouds, with the yellow light of the fire playing on it, until the barns in turn seemed to be on fire.

The two sat still for a long time. The wind carried gusts of heat to them over the floor. They could hear the far end of the building, as half burned rafters crashed, and let down the roofs above them, and with every fall there was a louder roar of the fire.

She pressed closer and closer to Traynor. He, with his arm around her, looked steadfastly above her head. There was fear in him, but there was also a dim delight unlike anything he had ever known, a full and quiet ecstasy.

"Back there," she said, "if I could throw the months away . . . then I'd be happy, Larry."

"What months?" he asked.

"Those after I left you, and when I was getting to know Parker."

"He was worth knowing."

"Do you mean that?"

"He was the greatest man I ever met," said Traynor solemnly.

"Larry, have you forgiven him out of the bottom of your heart?"

"Aye, I forgive him."

"Then I do, also."

"When the fire comes over the room, Rose, shall we make a break for the open?"

"No. I'd rather take my chances here in the house."

"There's the rifle with plenty of bullets in it."

She looked sharply up at him. "Well, we'll stay and fight . . . ," she murmured, but then, having a momentary change of heart, said vehemently: "I can save you, Larry! There's still time for me to save you . . . if I go out and call to them. They'll take me . . . and they won't harm me. . . ."

"Hush," Traynor said.

She was still.

He added: "I saw Jim Wharton's face at the window. Do you think I'd let you go out to him? Maybe it's better this way."

A strange light began to enter the room. The low-flowing smoke, wind-driven, covered the ground, and the fire reflected from the top of it through the window, brighter than the light of the lamp. This tremulous and rosy glow made the girl as beautiful as an angel, to the eye of her lover.

As he looked at her, he said: "Poor Channing! Poor devil! He's out there thinking of this, Rose.

He's eating his heart out. He's half wishing to be back in here with us."

"I don't want to think of him," she said.

"He killed poor old Sam. I ought to hate him. If we both lived, I suppose I'd try to go on the trail after him. But this way, I understand him. I'm glad to think of him. If it's God that makes us, he put too much mind and not enough heart in Channing. That's all there is to it. God help him, and God forgive him!"

A voice shouted huskily, as if in fear: "Hey, all of you! Watch through that smoke. Watch through that smoke! They might sneak out that way through the smoke!"

"And we might!" cried the girl. "Look, Larry!"

There was a great crashing that shook the entire house—what was left of it. The walls of the kitchen leaned crookedly. Plaster fell in great chunks from the ceiling and seemed to drop noiselessly, so huge was the uproar of the fire. And the heat was intense. The flames could not be more than a room away. The door of the dining room rattled back and forth as though a hand were shaking the knob of it—a poor ghost striving vainly to get into the kitchen where the pair waited.

But out the window, Traynor could see hardly a thing. For the funnels of white smoke rushing away from the house filled the air and covered the ground toward the barns.

"Rose," he said, "there's a ghost of a chance. . . ."

He went to the dining room door and pulled it open. Before him, a wild furnace was roaring, tossing up a million-footed dance of flames. The heat seared his face, scorched his body through his clothes.

He jammed the door shut again.

"Half a minute," he said to the girl. "Have you got a handkerchief? Then wet it in that pitcher and tie it over your mouth and nose like this. You see?"

He used the bloody handkerchief of the doctor, unknotting it from around his throat, for the same purpose. Then he looked again, and saw the girl was masked in white. She furled up the lower lip of the mask and threw her arms around him. And he, pushing the handkerchief high on his head, took what well might be his last clear view of her.

They only looked, desperately, with great eyes. They did not touch their lips together because each was striving, in divine despair, to see the face before them as it might be transfigured in another life.

They took a few vital, rushing seconds, then they drew down the wet masks again and went out the door onto the porch,

The full heat of the conflagration struck them at once. And the sweep of the wind hurried them into the boiling columns of the smoke. He had her hand in his.

"Close your eyes . . . I'll guide!" he called at her ear, and jumped with her from the edge of the porch.

He had a deep breath of pure air in his lungs. He ran forward, straining his eyes through the smoke that burned them, until the breath was spent in his lungs. They were far from the house, by this time, and the dim outline of a barn loomed dark before him.

He threw himself flat on the ground and dragged the girl down beside him.

She was coughing and gasping. But there, close to the ground, it was possible to breathe, and fill the lungs with better air, for the smoke kept rising.

Voices were still shouting.

"Keep a watch! Keep a watch! What's passing there?"

Distantly a rifle crackled. Three shots—at some smoky phantom, no doubt—and then the firing ceased. But it was a good measure of the peril into which they were running.

"Now," he said at the ear of Rose Laymon, and helped her to rise.

His knees were very weak, very weak. Yet he could stagger again into a run that carried them on toward the barns. The door of one yawned open right before them. He had carried the rifle slung in his left hand, so far. Now he transferred it to the right, and as he did so, he saw forms looming in the shadows of the doorway, peering into the smoke.

"Halt!" yelled one. The voice was a scream. "Here they come! Here!"

Traynor fired from the ready straight at the breast of that big, bearded fellow.

He turned and jammed the muzzle of the rifle at the face of the second man, and the fellow staggered backward, screeching out something about his eyes, firing a revolver repeatedly at nothingness.

The girl and Traynor already were far down the empty aisle of the barn, with flickering lights from the burning house entering the place.

Behind them, they heard a great crashing, a loud whistling of the triumphant wind, and a gust of heat and light streamed with a thousand-fold brilliance into the shadows of the barn.

That was what enabled them to see a half dozen horses tethered to the manger near the rear door. The frightened beasts were rearing and stamping and pulling violently back on the tie ropes to escape.

Rose Laymon threw up her hands in helpless terror as she saw that mill of great, tigerish bodies and heard the stamping of the hoofs, and saw the frantic eyes of the horses rolling toward the distant fire.

But Traynor, with a knife, cut loose the first two horses. They looked no better than ordinary broncos, but ordinary broncos would have to do. They could not pick and choose. He hung onto the reins of a fiery little pinto as Rose swung into the saddle.

She had the rear door of the barn open the next moment, and Traynor was barely able to hook a leg over the cantle of the saddle before his horse flew like a stone through the doorway and into the open night.

"This way! This way!" a voice was screeching. "This way, everyone! There they go . . . and on horse! Ride like hell! She's worth a hundred thousand to us. A thousand bucks to the gent that snags her first!"

Traynor, righting himself with a vast effort in the saddle, shot his horse in pursuit of the flying pinto. He heard behind him the swift beginning of the pursuit, the rumble of hoofs growing louder and louder as man after man joined the chase.

XI

They went up the easy slope of a hill which was half white with the moon, half trembling with the glow from the fire. The house of John Laymon lay prone, but huge red and yellow ghosts rose above it, dancing, sometimes throwing up great arms that disappeared in the upper air.

There was plenty of light for shooting, and the Whartons used it.

"Get that damned Traynor and the gal will give up!" the familiar voice of Jim Wharton was thundering.

And the result was an endless shower of bullets. Many of them flew wide. He only knew of their passing by the clicking of them through the branches of the trees or by the solid thudding of them into the trunks. But others clipped the air close about him, whining small with eagerness, each like a dog that misses its stroke and has to rush on past the quarry.

They rounded the hill. They entered a narrow shoot of a glade that carried them straight out into the road for Little Snake. To have that road under them seemed to ensure freedom from fear. He saw the head of the girl go up; he heard her crying: "We're going to make it, Larry! They're not going to catch us!"

But he, glancing back while he was still smiling, saw that half a dozen riders had forged ahead of the rest and were gaining steadily.

"Ride on, Rose!" he shouted at her.

She looked back in terror and cried out in dismay.

"Ride ahead!" he commanded. "You're lighter than I am. The pinto's a flash. You'll get to help first. I'll dodge away, somewhere. . . ."

She shook her head. She waved her absolute denial. And as he stared at her, the blood slowly trickling again from the open wound in his neck, he realized that she would never leave him—not now—not hereafter.

There are fools, he thought, who doubt the future. These are the men who have never gone through the fear of death with a friend in the knowledge that an equal faith is on each side, but for such as have endured the crisis, there must be a promise of life thereafter.

An eternity of faith poured over him as he watched her at his side and saw the tight pull she was keeping on the head of the pinto. She could flash away from him in an instant, but all the dangers in the world could never persuade her.

They rushed around a great loop of the road, and behind them the beating of the hoofs was louder and louder. Then voices raised in a sudden triumph that was like a song.

He looked wildly behind him, and saw the waving arms in the moonlight and the brandishing of bright guns.

He could not understand, until he looked ahead again and saw a solitary rider, straight up in the saddle, rushing his horse down a slope to intercept their way.

Would he come on them in time to stop them?

It seemed almost an even race, but at the end, as the pinto and Traynor's mustang struggled up a slope in the way, it seemed that the horse of the stranger was losing speed. He did not attempt to shoot. Perhaps he was afraid of striking the girl with a bullet. And Traynor himself held his fire with the rifle.

A roar of angry surprise rose from the road of the leading pursuers.

Then a twist of the way cut off everything from the view of Traynor. He was amazed to hear an outburst of rifle fire, with yells of high dismay scattered through the explosions.

The beat of hoofs died out. Still the voices clamored furiously, far away. Still the gunfire beat more and more rapidly.

But the pursuit had died at that spot.

What had happened? Well, he could save his breath for the work of riding, for he was very, very tired. And his legs shuddered against the sides of his horse, and his back was bending.

• • •

Hours seemed to flow past him, and more hours. He passed into a sort of trance through which the quiet, cheerful voice of the girl ate into his consciousness, from time to time. She was riding the pinto close to his horse. She was supporting him. And then he saw the lights of Little Snake clustered ahead.

They seemed to swarm in and out like hiving bees.

"Do you know what happened back there?" she asked him as she gave the horses their last halt before the town.

"Where?" he asked, his mind very dim.

"The rider who came down the slope . . . didn't you know him, Larry?"

"Ah, the fellow who almost cut us off . . . and then his horse petered out, or his nerve failed him?"

"His horse didn't give out . . . he has as much nerve as any man in the world."

"What do you mean, Rose?"

"It was Parker Channing. I knew him by the way he sat the saddle. I knew him by the wave of his hand when I looked back. And I saw him turning against the rest of them."

"The doctor? You mean that Channing cut in to help stop them? You mean . . . Rose, I've got to go back to him."

"Hush, and be still," said the girl. "He died

hours and hours ago They've killed him, and gone on. But not till he let us get safely away."

"Died? For us?" cried Traynor.

"Yes, for us," she answered.

And he knew that it was true. His brain cleared of all. He looked ahead at the twinkling lights of the town and the glimmering stars of the heaven, and it seemed to Traynor that the glory of the heavens descended without a check and overspread this earth.

Back there at the head of the hill, the doctor had charged in earnest to cut off the retreat of the two, for he felt that he had abandoned all shame and all virtue forever when he left the two in the condemned house of Laymon. There was nothing for him, now, but to face forward into crime and greater crime and welcome the darkness of the future.

And there was a savage earnestness in his riding as he considered how close the two rode together. Traynor beside the girl. He wanted to kill Traynor—not with guns, but with his hands. When the last life bubbled up under the compressed tips of his fingers, he would be satisfied, he told himself, and not until then.

What was it that had changed him? It was when he saw, quite clearly by the moonlight, how Rose Laymon was reining in her pinto until its neck bowed sharply. It was when he understood her will to live or die at the side of Traynor.

If his strength was in his mind rather than in his heart, perhaps it was in the quiet perfection of his thinking that he saw how the two were blended together for a single destiny that should be far higher than to be trampled down by the ruffians of Jim Wharton. And it was clear thinking, also, that showed him what he must do.

No one would know. His reputation would not be cleansed by the act, unless the girl, perhaps, had recognized him by his riding. But he had to face the Whartons and check their pursuit for a few vital minutes.

So, as he swung into the road at the crest of the shallow hill, he turned straight back toward the pursuers, and pulled his rifle out of its holster.

He took good aim. The very first shot jerked back the head of the foremost rider, and with upflung arms the man dropped backward out of the saddle. The second brought a yell of agony.

The party split to this side and to that, and with screaming curses the riders fled for cover.

He could ride after the fugitive pair, now. But that was not his plan. To his clear brain the future of this act was very plain. His life was cast away. He had thrown it away and made it forfeit with the bullet that killed old Sam. Perhaps he had returned a partial payment by the slaying of the ruffian, who lay yonder, twisted in the road. But there was still more to do—it was a long account.

He got his horse into a nest of rocks and made the animal lie down.

By that time, the tail of the pursuit had come up, and warning yells of the Whartons made the other men take cover. They began to spread to this side and to that. Bullets, now and then, whirred through his imperfect fortifications.

He kept a keen look-out.

He saw a shadow crawling between the bushes, took careful aim, and fired. The man leaped up with a yell that burned like a torch through the brain of the doctor. One bound, and the fellow was out of sight.

But he would remember this night the rest of his days.

Suddenly, on his right, four men charged right up the hill for him.

They came from a distance of fifteen yards, only.

He dropped, one, two—and the remaining pair dodged to the side and pitched out of view behind an outcrop of rock.

One of the other two lay still. The second, screaming, got to his hands and knees, and started crawling away.

The doctor let him crawl. Something in the tone of that groaning told him that the bullet wound was through the body, and if that were the case . . .

In the meantime, the pair under the rock so close at hand would be a thorn in his flesh. He had to keep his attention at least half for them.

Still he watched until he saw a head and shoulders lift from beside the rock. He had to snatch up his own rifle to shoot quickly. He fired.

He knew that his bullet struck the target. The head bobbed down like a weighted cork, but right through the shoulder and into the body of the doctor drove the answering slug.

That was his end, and he knew it.

Calmly—because there was the clear mind in him to the end—he prepared for the last stroke.

He could not manage the rifle very well with one arm. But he had a borrowed Wharton revolver. That was in his hand as he roused the horse and slipped into the saddle.

The instant his silhouette loomed, the rapid firing began. He spurred the mustang straight toward the flashes of the guns. And a glory came over the doctor, and enlarged his spirit, and widened his throat, and the shout that came from him was like a single note from a great song.

So, firing steadily, aiming his shots, he drove his charge home against his enemy until a bullet, mercifully straight, struck the consciousness from him, and loosed the life from the body, and sent the unharmed spirit winging on its way.

They gave Parker Channing a church funeral. And the town of Little Snake followed him to the grave.

There was a very odd picture of Rose Laymon kneeling at the edge of the grave, dropping roses into it. The rest of the people held back. They knew it was her right, her duty, to play the part of chief mourner. And not a soul in Little Snake doubted that her tears were real.

Those who watched kept shifting their looks from the girl to the pale-faced, solemn young man who stood not far behind her, with his head bowed. He was waiting for the end of the ceremony. He was waiting for Rose Laymon. And it is fair to say that in all of Little Snake there was not a man who did not judge that Larry Traynor had come fairly by his happiness.

LUCK AND A HORSE

I

The voice with its usual nasal whine, cut into his sleep: "Margie! Margie!"

As much as he detested the sound, he was glad to be called away from the storm and wasteland of his dreaming. First of all, when he wakened in the attic, there was the smell of rats. It choked him. Then through the skylight he saw the two stars—a big yellow one above, and a meager companion trembling beneath it. He told himself again, for the thousandth time, that he would take a look at those stars as soon as he was out in the open and write them down in his memory so that he could find the names in an almanac or wherever it was that one located stars. He had always forgotten, but this morning he would remember.

"Margie! Oh, Margie!"

That was the custom of Sylvester Train, always to lie abed and call to his niece without anger, making a virtue of his patience until she had moved. Tommy Grant listened as always with breathless suspense, and in the dark of the autumn morning it was like soul calling to soul through the disembodied words to do something about it. He should not permit the poor girl to be suffering again. He should act that instant, before the growled response came from her.

But he knew that he would not act. As he had done a thousand times before. So now he would simply lie there, trembling with the lack of spirit, with his heart aching high in his throat.

"Margie! Mar-*gie!* Oh, Margie!"

"Yess!" came the far-off sigh of pain.

"Time to get up! Margie . . . time to get up."

"Y-e-s," more faintly.

When the sun rises, mortals should be at work, Uncle Sylvester Train always said. That meant at work in the fields, but the preparations should all be made before. When *he* was a boy, back in Iowa, many a time he was in the field so early that the moonlight was brighter than the dawn. Wise men live a hundred years in fifty, by doubling the length of their daily labor. Sluggards never live at all, said Uncle Sylvester.

"Margie! Oh, Margie!"

He made the call sharper, barking it out— but still without malice in the sound, or anger. Simply the patient barking of a faithful soul who will rouse the household in time.

"Yes, oh, yes! Just leave me alone a minute, while I wake up!" cried Margie, with fury and sorrow in her voice.

Tommy Grant sat erect in his bed. It was always at this point that he roused himself suddenly and sat for a moment, even in the frost of winter, with his pulses stronger and faster.

A voice came shouting up in him: *Let her alone, Train! Let her sleep. Damn you . . . damn you . . . you fat, lazy bully . . . you let her sleep!*

That shouting voice swelled his throat, parted his lips, but died in a mere tremor of his lips, that whispered: "I'm no good. I'm just a coward. Nobody knows what a yellow coward I am. I'd take water from a child!"

"Margie! Oh, Mar-*gie!*"

"Yes, yes, yes, yes!"

Clearly, Tommy could hear the rustle of the covers thrown back, the creak of the springs as she sat up, and then the moaning yawn as she stretched her arms.

Blear-eyed, with her red hair in a tangle, there she would sit for a moment, till the despair and the cold of the morning had finally roused her to the day's work. That despair, and her uncle's voice, saying very quietly, now: "Are you up, Margie? Are you up, girl? Time to be up and stirring, Margie."

"I *am* up!" snapped Margie, and her heels hit the floor like two drumbeats on a drum.

Tommy Grant slid from bed also, for when the cook is up, the day has fairly begun on anybody's ranch. He pulled off the nightgown he was wearing and hugged his shivering body. He could feel the gooseflesh roughening his skin, but only gradually could he bring his mind back to the end of the day before.

Old Train had been talking until ten-thirty about his hero, Danton, how he had died, how he had said to himself—"No weakness, Danton"—as he climbed to the guillotine. He had shown them a picture of Danton, and the face was almost a likeness of Uncle Sylvester himself—it was so full of fat and muscle.

At ten-thirty Tommy Grant had climbed the stairs.

"Good night, sleep tight, don't let the rats bite!" Train called out at the sounds of the footsteps.

Tommy Grant had hung the lantern from a nail on the middle rafter. That was it.

Now he found the lantern. The rust of it had an oily feeling from the kerosene. Even when there is no actual leak, kerosene will seep through any screw-lid or corked vent. He pushed down the side wires; the chimney rose with a dreary screech. Then he had to search for a match while he grew colder and colder. He found the chair beside his bed. The half-filled sack of Bull Durham rustled under his touch; the package of wheat-straw papers was there, too, but not the matches. He kneeled on the splintery floor and fell about until he found the little cube of the sulphur matches. He stood up with them, recalling that once in the bunkhouse of the Kramer Ranch, he had seen old Vince Purvis light a sulphur match by scratching it on the bare hide of his thigh. In spite of his chattering teeth, he grinned at the memory.

He lighted the lantern. The smell of the oily smoke joined that of the rats. As he reached for his clothes, and dressed, he tried not to see what the shadows covered in every corner, but he knew them too well to avoid being aware of the yellow-painted shafts for the worn-out buggy, the odd pieces of harness that hung from the roof tree, gathering dust and sustaining cobwebs, half a dozen blades for the mowing machine, worn beyond use but kept here to rust, because nothing was ever thrown away on this place. Sylvester Train would quote that little poem about the coward who broke his sword and threw it away, but the prince, disarmed, found that broken fragment and won a glorious field.

In one large box were kept broken carpenter tools; in a smaller box were remnants of the childhood of Margie—books with frayed cardboard covers, and colored pictures of dogs and playing youngsters, mutilated dolls, rusted toys. Tommy Grant had opened that box only once, in fact, but in his thought he re-opened it every day of his life and looked with pity at the junk. On what day of her life had Margie collected all these relics and wrapped them up, and put them neatly away? She was only about twenty, or so, even now. It made him feel a little sick. It made him feel as though he had been sleeping in a graveyard where only children are buried.

He took the lantern from its nail and went down the steep stairs. His clothes were damp. The stiff leather of his boots hurt his feet. He knew that someday he would have to do something about corns.

"Margie! Oh, Margie!"

The rattling at the kitchen stove ceased.

"Yes, Uncle?"

"Don't forget my coffee, Margie!"

He always reminded her, always.

She always answered: "All right, all right."

She had lighted the fire. She was putting the lids back above the firebox when he entered the kitchen, where heavy swirls of smoke, yellow and white, moved in the air of the room like oil through water. She was wearing a blue gingham dress that buttoned down the back. She had buttoned it crookedly. The whole dress hung awry from her shoulders.

" 'Morning, Margie," he said.

She bent hastily over the wood box as she answered.

He lingered at the door for an instant, as she seemed to be hunting for the right piece of wood. Finally, he went out into the dark of the morning.

Margie had not been looking for the right piece of wood. It was simply that she never would look him in the face before she had washed thoroughly, and made herself neat. She was funny about that.

When he would come back from the barn, she would be willing enough to look at him, and she would be in order, too. Today she would discover that her dress was buttoned crookedly down the back, and be embarrassed.

Women are odd, thought Tommy Grant.

Just the gray edge of the morning was getting between the mountains and the upper night. Mount Sullivan and The Arrowhead were blacker than paint, but, between them, Comanche Pass focused whatever light there was—just a bright spot, like looking down a clean gun barrel.

He held up his hand. There was a bit of a breeze, still blowing out of the cold and the mystery of night. He unhooked the lever of the windmill. The long wire sprang jangling up; the fan turned with a long, groaning note; the wheel began to turn; the pump sucked vainly for half a dozen strokes, then raised the water and the foolish, chuckling noise began, the rhythmic plumping of the stream as it fell into the long horse troughs.

He went to the corral gate, tall and ugly as a gibbet. The locking bar was rough—someday he would have to plane it smooth. There are a lot of things to think of on a ranch. You do one thing, but there are ten more waiting.

It was cold. He should have put on a coat.

He stepped to the ankle in foul mud, and stood there a moment before freeing his foot, smiling with sardonic understanding at his fate. He cast the lantern light over the slimy face of the ground and nodded. His understanding was deeper than ever.

He hauled at the handle of the barn door. It stuck. He had slammed it hard, the night before, and one of the runners had jumped the track above. Now he had to lift the clumsy weight, carefully, and hold it suspended with his aching shoulder until the wheel was exactly over the track. It missed the close fit. He had to raise it again, and again. And the wind was cold. It was like splashing ice water on his stomach. Anybody that's not a fool, who would want to live on a ranch?

At last he could haul the door open. He gave it a good thrust and heard it run back with soft thunder. Then the warmth, the sweet smell of the hay came out to him. He raised the lantern, saw the line of lifted heads, the pricking ears, the light glittering from eye to eye. They whinnied. Every one of them whinnied, except the brown colt at the end of the row. He merely jammed his breast against the manger so that he could lift his head higher to watch his master.

Nine horses in a row, and eight of them calling to him, and one of them waiting for his touch. The hay bulged out between the pillars of the mow; it was two-thirds full of the best volunteer oats and wheat. The huge feed box was brimming with crushed barley. He threw back the lid of the bin and the fragrance of the grain made his mouth water. Eight horses calling to him, and the brown colt waiting.

He had two measuring tins, which meant four trips to feed the eight, and a special trip to feed the brown colt. He made the four trips. The bay mare, he noticed, no longer tried to jam out the bottom of the grain box. He noted this grimly, remembering how he had broken her of that habit by putting rocks in with the barley, one day. It was cruel, but some fools have to be taught with cruelty.

Gray Mike filled his mouth from his portion, and then turned his head and looked with contented eyes toward Tommy, all the while dribbling away half the mouthful of precious grain.

"You fool. You old wall-eyed, bleary fool . . . look what you're doing!" shouted Tommy Grant. He was furious. Then he noticed the hollows above the eyes of Mike, hollows in which the muscles were bulging in and sinking as he chewed. Poor Mike was growing old and slow on the run, but whenever a grade came, he showed all the rest how to pull, and at plow he was a steady engine, all day long. He was descended from the older generation, when the West was filled with great men and great horses.

Tommy Grant made the fifth trip, but instead of taking only the one can for the brown colt, he carried two, and emptied one of them in the feed box of Mike. The big, worn, kind head turned toward him. He held his hand under the lips of Mike and kept the grain from dribbling away, and he was filled with a guilty sense of joy. It was as well that Sylvester Train did not know that two portions were given to any one horse.

At last he could go to the brown colt, his own horse. Brownie had watched all this time, not moving but trembling with joyous expectation.

"Get over! Get over, will you?" He jabbed Brownie in the ribs. "Here you are!"

He raised the measuring can high and let the barley shower down into the feed box, and as the grain ran, prickles and laughing tingles went up the back and over the scalp of Tommy Grant. For the colt paid no attention to the grain, but merely sniffed at his hands, impatiently. He reached out with a pawing hoof. He stamped. In a pretended fury, he lifted his head and nibbled at the man's hair.

Tommy choked. His lips trembled.

"You old fool! Why, you old fool," he said. "You don't know anything. You're just an old fool, is what you are."

He scooped up some of the grain in the palm of his hand. Brownie caught the whole width of the hand between his teeth, gently. Then he took up the barley. The twitching of his upper lip tickled the skin. Only when every grain was gone would he go on to start his morning meal.

Tommy Grant stood by and watched.

"Look what kind of a fool you are. You'd starve, if I didn't come around. I can't waste all my time on you. You're no good. You're not a damned bit of good!"

He ran his hand down the neck of the colt. It was velvet. It was silk laid thinly on over the ripple and flow of the muscles. The colt, instantly, raised his head from the barley.

"Look . . . you're not a horse. You're a cat. You'd rather be petted than eat. You're a big worthless cat."

He removed his hand, and as Brownie began to munch again, he stood by, no longer caressing the horse with his touch but with his thought.

Anyone that's not a fool—who would want to live in a city? Nine stalled horses, nine infants in a row, some good, some mischievous, some dull, some wise, but all, since the coming of Tommy Grant, working better for the touch of his voice than for the stroke of any whip.

He climbed into the mow, wading knee-deep in the wealth of the hay while he shoved down the feed into the mangers. He climbed back out, and began the currying and brushing. He finished that and harnessed all except the bay mare, for she had a bad sore near the top of her shoulder. He had cut out some of the stuffing of the collar pad, but still the sore grew worse, and she ought to be rested.

The heart of Tommy Grant sank. For he knew that when Sylvester Train heard this, he would order the brown colt to be put into harness.

Well, if it came to that pinch, he, Tommy Grant, would tell Sylvester Train a few honest truths about himself. No matter what happened, he would tell him a few facts—and then, no matter what happened.

This is a free country, isn't it?

II

When he got outside of the barn, again, he saw that there was no need of carrying the lantern, for the morning had advanced to such brightness that he could see the plow standing on the hillside in the midst of the forty-acre land which he was working on. He could see the iron double trees stretched out before the plow, and the blackbirds were beginning where they had left off at darkness the day before. Where black furrows had not run, the stubble was a dirty yellow mist. It had rained in the night and it might rain again during the day, for a thunderhead rose in the west from the dusky shadow of the earth to the brightness of the upper morning, like an island whose roots slope down into the dark sea.

He blew out the lantern and went on through a new loneliness to the house, where the smoke was fuming busily out of the kitchen chimney. The white leghorns were out, scratching about the door, when he pumped a basin of cold water, worked up a lather with the yellow laundry soap, and scrubbed himself. Then he stood at the broken bit of mirror that was nailed against the house and combed his hair. Sylvester Train believed that working men ought to make their toilets outside of the house. In harvest time, in haying, one doesn't want to have a troop of louts wandering about through the house. The home of a gentleman is his castle, and without privacy the soul cannot live.

Tommy Grant thought of these sayings as he combed his hair. He was always remembering the speeches of Sylvester Train. But on this morning he was aware with new eyes of his own face.

Suppose that Train asked for the brown colt in the team—well, this is a free country, isn't it? And Tommy was twenty-five. He frowned and turned his head a little because he thought it made him look older. He might pass for thirty, anywhere. He was not much to look at. To make up his six feet and an inch his body had been stretched, and it had given in some parts more than others. In the neck, for instance. He had a rather round face with high cheek bones; there was not much nose, but plenty of mouth. When he walked, his head nodded a bit so that strangers sometimes thought that he was recognizing them, and doing it too casually. When he looked into a mirror, he always frowned to gain dignity, but when he was among his fellows he felt that he had an open-eyed goose look.

Turning to the kitchen door, he waved his hand, but the chickens moved only leisurely from his path. That's the trouble. When people or things got used to you, they take you for granted. It's easy to get into such a rut that your head never shows above the edge of it; people take you as a matter of course; what you really are is lost in the dull of every day.

Then he stood by the kitchen stove, warming his hands over the smoke and heat of it. His fingernails and the callous inside of his thumbs were soiled. He had scrubbed them with the brush, but cold water is not a good solvent, and axle grease and such stuff works right into the skin. However, he put his hands into the pockets of his overalls because Margie was a stickler about cleanliness. She noticed everything. When she got to be middle-aged, maybe she would be a nagger.

She had opened the oven door. A burst of thick smoke flew out at her, and while she frowned, peering in at the state of the biscuits, he took a good look at her. She had a dish towel in her hand. She was wearing rubber gloves. But he could hardly tell how she looked.

He was inclined to look away from her toward his memory of what she had been at the dance last Saturday when she wore the green dress and Bert Ellis had asked her to dance three times. That fellow Ellis was a jailbird, but he was a slick one and the girls were crazy about him. He was always smiling, always easy-going. Nobody could dance like Bert Ellis, but she had accepted him only once.

"Why?" Tommy Grant had asked her.

"I'm tired. I'd rather sit out with you, Tommy," she had said.

But that had not been all of her reason.

You take even a poor little drudge like Margie, who has to dress all up before she looks like anything—even a girl like that can talk mysteriously, and seem to be around the corner from you, if you understand.

He considered this fact, as he stared down through the fumes of cookery at the bacon that was stirring and bubbling in its own fat, at the sliced potatoes which were turning brown. He wondered why his heart was so heavy. But then he remembered about the sore shoulder of the bay mare—he remembered about the brown colt. You shouldn't work a four-year-old in a plow team. The steady lugging may spoil its shoulder. Hauling on the road isn't so bad, but plowing is no good. There's no let-up to it.

"Margie," he said.

She closed the oven door and stood up quickly, smiling at him. He was about to tell her of the problem concerning Brownie. She would understand, but, after all, she had troubles enough of her own, getting up at the crack of dawn and working all day long. He made a great effort, and controlled his speech.

"What's the matter?" she asked.

"Nothing," he said. "It was just . . . nothing."

"You're all tied up in knots about something,"

said Margie. "Go on, Tommy. You'll tell me, sooner or later . . . why not now?"

"I love you, Margie. That's all."

His brain could not believe his own voice, but now that the thing had been said, the truth of it rang and re-echoed through all the corridors of his soul. He had always loved her. Of course he had. Even when he first came there to work, four years before, though that had been a time when she still giggled a good deal, and she was only sixteen. What made him love her? It was a way she had of flashing out through the dreary mist of things, the way a window flames in sunrise or sunset—the flame is always golden.

"You love me?" she was saying. "Oh, Tommy."

She hurried up to him with her hands gripped and made a gesture from her breast to his.

"You love me? Oh, Tommy!"

She turned straight away and went to the sink, where she rattled pans.

Tommy Grant looked at the open door which led to the dining room, for Sylvester Train—his morning cup of coffee drained—might now be sitting at the dining room table, waiting patiently, smiling and sneering at his own thoughts.

What she had said kept working further and deeper in him, and how she had looked. One might have called it derision, except for the breaking of her voice.

She was back at the stove, opening the oven

again, hauling out the great black baking pan that contained the biscuits. No one could make better sour-milk biscuits. She knocked the pan on the edge of the table, and made the biscuits shower out into a clean dish cloth. That kitchen was always full of dish towels, always clean.

She stepped back to the stove barely in time to rescue the coffee as the lid of the pot lifted above a frothing yellow.

"You might have an eye," she said crossly.

Just after he had told her that he loved her, she could say a thing like that! "I love you." What more can a man say to a girl? But it was over her shoulder and forgotten in an instant.

"Take these in," she commanded.

He accepted the warmed platter on which the biscuits were heaped. They always had biscuits. Sylvester Train ate heaps of them, with molasses and plenty of butter. But as Tommy was about to carry his platter into the dining room, she laid a hand on his arm and looked up into his face with desperate eyes, for an instant—not as a girl at her lover, but as a mother at a child for which her hopes are not quite as great as her knowledge. Then she let him go, and he went with a frowning brow and a weak heart into the dining room.

She had no right to look at him in such a way. What did she know?

Sylvester Train saw him coming and parted his mustache with the first and second fingers of his left hand. He only smoked cigars on Sundays, but, nevertheless, there remained a yellow stain in the center of that pale mustache.

"So you're getting to be a handy man around the house, are you, Tommy? You know what John A. Creevy said about handy men about the house?"

"No," admitted Tommy Grant.

He spoke with anger and with volume, but, as usual, he was overlooked.

Sylvester Train drew a notebook from his pocket, opened it to a blank page, took out a flat carpenter's pencil, and started drawing lines carefully.

"John A. Creevy," Sylvester Train announced, "said that a handy man about the house was never worth a damn outside of the house."

"I wanted to tell you about the bay mare," said Tommy Grant. He was glad that he had been insulted. He was glad of the brave warmth that was growing up in his heart. "I wanted to tell you about the mare, because . . ."

"If you've washed your hands, sit down to breakfast," said Train. "John A. Creevy said that a good hot breakfast is half the day's work."

Train's niece came in with the other things. She sat down and looked about the table with an anxious eye.

"Nothing but the mustard," said her uncle.

She jumped up at once. "I'm always forgetting,"

she cried, and hurried for the mustard pot.

Sylvester Train ate mustard with his fried bacon.

Tommy Grant was in a muse. She had said: "You love me? Oh, Tommy!" Well, that was all right. Girls are odd. You can never know what they'll do next. But when she touched his arm and looked desperately up into his face . . . why you might have thought that she was his grandmother or something. And she was only twenty.

"Did you feel the house shake last night, when the thunderstorm hit us?" Margie asked as she came back and slipped into her chair again.

"*He* didn't hear," said Sylvester Train. "He was snoring through it all. I was lying awake, but it wasn't about the thunderstorm that I was thinking, Margie. Not about that!"

He shook his head, and his thin, pale hair rose a bit and flopped about his head like a small halo. In the meantime, he was finishing building a forkful in the English style, composing it of bacon, mustard, potatoes, with salt and pepper added. He lowered his head. His mouth opened wide, swayed sideways . . .

The fascinated eyes of Tommy and Margie were wrenched away from this spectacle of effort and skill, and their glances met, partly in horror, partly in amusement.

"What did you say about the bay mare?" asked the girl.

"She's got a sore shoulder."

"Pick out the stuffing of the shoulder pad. How many times have I to show you how to do that?" mumbled Sylvester Train.

A flood of coffee helped to empty his mouth. He tapped his forefinger on the table to hold attention while he caught his breath.

"You have to learn to do things. You won't always have such an easy job at a good place like this, young man!"

"I've picked the stuffing out of the pad."

"Did you put on the tar ointment?"

"No."

"I told you always to put on the tar ointment. I told you always to!" He bumped the table with his hand. "Damn!" said Sylvester Train. "You'd make even John A. Creevy swear."

"The veterinary says the tar ointment is no good," Tommy Grant tried to explain to his employer.

"Why no good?"

"It sort of burns the skin."

"What veterinary?"

"Doc Walters."

"That young fool?"

"You said he was the best veterinary in the county. You said so last week."

"Times change, and men with them," said Sylvester Train, with the voice of Jupiter.

It was no good arguing with Train. Everybody

knew that he never had been downed in an argument. If you backed him against a wall, he'd simply kick the wall down, or jump over it.

"Well, the mare has a sore shoulder. I've doctored her for a week, but the shoulder's worse."

"For a week? Why didn't you tell me about it sooner?"

Calmly, darkly, the boy stared at the fat man as Train swayed from side to side in his chair with passion in his face.

"I'm never told until it's too late," Sylvester Train complained. "Second thought is generally too late, said John A. Creevy. And you have nothing but second thoughts. Why didn't you tell me before?"

Tommy Grant set his teeth and said through them: "She's got a sore shoulder. She'll have to be laid out of team for a week . . . maybe two weeks. I don't know."

"Lay a good, sound horse up because it's got a bit of a sore on one shoulder? Lay it up for a week? Napoleon never would have seen the sunny plains of Italy if he'd stopped every time a horse had a sore. What did Danton say? 'Audacity! Audacity! Always audacity!' That was when France was trembling before the armies of united Europe. You talk to me about a horse with a sore shoulder . . . bah!"

The boy laid down his knife and fork.

"You want me to work her . . . sore shoulder or not . . . do you?" he asked.

"Of course he doesn't," Margie said instantly. She had recognized the final note of danger. It seldom came from Tommy Grant, and when it did, it was so softly sounded that she was always afraid that her uncle would overlook it. If Tommy went, where else would Sylvester Train find a man willing to work more for hope than for wages. Besides . . .

"Of course he doesn't," Margie repeated. "He was simply arguing a point. Uncle Sylvester wouldn't torture a dumb beast. Don't be silly, Tommy. You know Uncle Sylvester wouldn't be cruel."

"If the bay mare can't work, put in the brown colt," said Train.

With the same despair, rage, but sober gravity, Tommy Grant regarded his employer. He could swear that he would lay down his life sooner than surrender the point, but he could also swear that in some manner, Train would gain his end.

"A great fat hulk of a brute," said Train, "that eats its head off all day long."

"You take twelve dollars a month off my pay every month to feed that horse."

"By the merciful heavens, you grain it, too . . . you grain a stall-bound, worthless, fat-sided fool of a colt . . . and now you don't want it to work!"

"I own that horse."

"A good thing you do. I wouldn't have it."

"You thought differently when you held up six months of my wages to pay for it."

Sylvester Train struck the table. The tableware jumped and crashed back down with a clang.

"What are you looking for?" he thundered. "Trouble? Is that it? Trouble? Is that what you want?"

A wave of cold dashed over Tommy Grant. He saw that the girl was looking down at the table, pain in her face, and then he remembered the despair with which she had looked up at him in the kitchen.

That was it. She knew that he was a coward.

"I'm not afraid of any trouble you can make!" he shouted wildly.

He saw the girl wince. Well, why? He had spoken right out. What more could she want?

"An old man and a cripple . . . you're not afraid of any trouble that *he* can make for you!" said Sylvester Train. "Well, well, well! There was a time when you might have felt differently. There was a time when I lifted Riley Ogden and Ralph Hughes off their feet. Well, those days are gone. John A. Creevy says that many a man is dead before his death day, and John A. Creevy is right. *I* am dead. My body is dead. As a ghost I sit at the table. I speak, and no man regales me. Thought remains when the body is nothing, but what is thought in this world? A cipher! At my own table . . . where John A. Creevy has sat like the lion that he was . . . ah, God . . . when men were men . . . when men . . ."

He paused. One hand gripped his breast deeply. His head was raised to the unforgotten ghosts of the other days.

Tommy Grant was stunned. He had been overwhelmed by rhetoric and John A. Creevy before, but never so utterly destroyed.

"Look," he said faintly. "What I mean is that Brownie is only four years old."

Sylvester Train did not look. He dropped his forehead, with an audible thud into the palm of his left hand and stared at his plate.

"Brownie could work," said Tommy Grant. "I don't mean that he couldn't work. Only, plowing's too heavy for him. He hasn't the shoulders of a work horse. With shoulders that slope like his . . . heavy, steady lugging . . ."

Sylvester Train shook his head wearily, and with his fork jabbed at a bit of bacon, which he raised to his lips.

"I can't work Brownie in the plow team. I'd haul with him."

"How much does Brownie weigh?"

The softness of this voice warned Grant that something lay behind in ulterior meanings, but nevertheless he answered.

"About eleven hundred."

"Eleven hundred pounds?"

"What else could the 'eleven hundred' mean? Yes," said Tommy Grant.

"Eleven hundred pounds, but he can't work in a plow team?"

"He's got sloping shoulders that . . ."

Sylvester Train, having conveyed a forkful of potatoes, bacon, and a dab of mustard to his mouth, raised the fork for a moment of mastication, and to halt all further traffic in words.

Then he said: "Never mind. He's your horse. You can do what you please with him. I can't *force* you to work him. I can lay up the bay and another horse as well. You can work with three spans, only, while the brown colt eats more good hay and barley and waits for the time when he's to bear the king's son!"

Sylvester Train's plate was empty. He pushed it disdainfully from him and turned his head to look out the window.

"The king's son," he said, with a sneer and a heave of his head and shoulders.

There was nothing, however, on which Tommy could seize. There was nothing he could use. He looked anxiously toward the girl, to see what she expected of him, and was relieved when she shook her head.

"Well, throw on a hundred sacks and haul them to town," said Train in disgust. "Perhaps the brown colt can help, there. You say that he can haul on the road, and a hundred sacks is a light load. I don't want to overstrain the colt. I wouldn't do that. Perhaps you will use him. If not, take three spans and break their hearts. I leave it to you."

"If you go to town, will you get me some rubber gloves, Tommy?" asked the girl. She made her voice light. She felt that she was relieving a strain.

"Sure I will," said Tommy.

"Get her some what?" asked Train.

"Some rubber gloves," said Tommy.

"Rubber gloves?"

"Yes."

"Rubber for what?" Train shouted.

"Why should she wear her hands out?" Tommy asked.

"Young man, you express yourself clearly, with beautiful choice of words, with language that would have moved John A. Creevy to admiration, but, at the present moment, I am addressing my niece, and though her education does not match yours, does not compare, perhaps she will be able to answer for herself."

"It's the dish water and things like that, Uncle Sylvester. That's what softens a girl's nails and makes them break."

"Ah, it softens the nails?"

"Yes. And then the water wrinkles the skin."

"Ah, it wrinkles the skin?"

"Yes, you know. . . ."

"Did your mother ever use rubber gloves?"

"No, but . . ."

"Did her mother before her ever use rubber gloves?"

"No, but you see rubber wasn't known to be . . ."

"Never mind, never mind. Rubber gloves you want, and rubber gloves you must have. 'Our wastage of money and time, our trifling mechanical devices which we call civilization,' as John A. Creevy used to say. To a starving nation, the women say . . . 'Let us have rubber gloves.' Those were other days, and that was another race, when the terrible voice of Danton sounded, and the men and the women of a great nation rose to strike for the liberation of the human race. Those were other days!"

He sank his head on his hands once more.

"Don't bother about the gloves, Tommy," said the girl.

He looked across the table at her hands, slender, smooth, beautifully made. It seemed to him that he had never seen them before, but that he had always loved her because of them.

"I'll get you the gloves . . . I'll buy them myself," he said.

Sylvester Train did not hear. He was shaking a mournful head, and as he contemplated the glories of the past, he casually speared a slice of bacon, and conveyed it not to his plate, but to his lips.

III

Tommy Grant went out to the wood pile to smoke his after-breakfast cigarette and sat on the chopping block. That was a favorite place because the newly chopped wood had a pleasant fragrance, and he could smoke while he watched the sun rising beyond Comanche Pass. The towering thunderhead had melted into a disordered throng of clouds, all rolling smoke below and bright fire above. It looked as though the rain might hold off.

With half his mind he watched the morning grow. The other half pondered on Margie and the strangeness of her words. Now that he was in the open and looked back toward the darkness of the dining room it seemed to him that he could understand—she had meant that they were both lost in the grasp of Sylvester Train and that they would only be more completely involved by a marriage that would tie them together in the bondage of their present way of life. At least, perhaps that was what she meant. But girls are strange, and one never can tell.

He finished his cigarette, stood up, and ground the butt under his heel. Before he left the place that morning, he would ask Train to write him a check for his month of arrears in pay. That was a good, solid sum. A chunk of money to start on.

He went to the barn, untied the horses, turned them out to water, drove them back again to their places. Then he harnessed Brownie. He had bought that harness himself, and it was the best and lightest on the place.

The collar was made-to-order. The pad was deep and soft, filled with culled horsehair. The projecting tops of the haims were tipped with brass, and more brass flamed about the bridle and the harness saddle. He combed out the forelock and stepped back to squint at the picture.

Well, Brownie looked worthy of bearing a king's son. He was both beautiful and fierce in seeming. As he stood there with his head up, he appeared ready to bound into the air—yes, and stride upon it! He would put the colt on the near point, just ahead of old Gray Mike. In that way, nothing could go wrong.

He took out the team, hauled two wagons from the big shed, coupled them together, hitched the eight, and then drove around the corral to the granary on the farther side. Old Bird, the jerk-line leader, stepped out with full fire, glad of this day off from plowing. She kept the fifth chain taut, and the whole team trotted, with Brownie dancing on his toes until the heart of the driver danced also. Behind him, the two empty wagons rattled and roared. He made a good turn and pulled up flush with the granary door.

It was open. Sylvester Train was already there, stomping about with his heavy cudgel of a walking stick. He was chuckling with triumph. "No rats in here. Not a rat. Not a damned rat in here." He struck the floor with the cane. "Not a rat. You hear me, Tommy?"

For when Train decided, three years before, that he would store his grain at the end of the harvest season and sell only when the prices were higher, his neighbors had vowed that rats and mice would riddle his sacks for him. But he had proved them wrong. He had proved Tommy Grant wrong, also. He bought a great quantity of five gallon oil tins and a pair of shears for cutting the stuff. Then they sheathed the whole bottom of the granary with tin, and all the sides, too, six feet from the ground. Besides that, they used poisoned grain to pick off stragglers which might come investigating the treasure trove whose scent blew down the wind and, finally, every day, or twice a day, Sylvester Train inspected his granary to make sure that depredations had not begun. Nothing pleased him so much as his success in this matter.

The sacks were piled eight high in the granary, and Tommy Grant began to load them rapidly. He put sixty sacks on the front wagon, and then he pulled up and laded the train with forty more. Train pretended to be paying little attention, but actually Tommy knew that his boss was there to

139

count the sacks and to make sure that the load was no larger than he had commanded. The sun came up through Comanche Pass while Tommy still was at work, and against the intolerable flare of light, he could see even the trees that fringed the mountain, like hair on an unshaven cheek.

With the wagons loaded, he roped down the sacks, tightening the ropes on the windlass that was set into the tail of each wagon.

"I'm the only man around here that thought of using 'em," declared Train. "Look at the time I save you, that way, and look at the work, too. Most of 'em tighten the ropes by twisting sticks in 'em. Twisting sticks," he added with a sneer.

"I'll be needing some money," said Tommy Grant.

"You drive on and stop at the house. There'll be a list of things for you to buy in town."

"What I mean about money," Tommy said, "I'd like to have the whole lot I'm owed. I might be needing to have everything up to date because . . ."

Train was closing the door of the granary, slamming it, grunting loudly and steadily. Now he pretended that he had not heard the last speech of his hired man.

"Hurry along to the house," he said. "You ought to have been rolling on the road by sunup."

"Load a hundred sacks and be on the road by sunup?" said Tommy Grant.

"Come now. Get moving!"

The anger of Tommy was so great that he shouted to his team without remembering for a moment that the brown colt was a part of it.

"Here!" yelled Sylvester Train. "Make that worthless fool pull its share. Make it . . ." He didn't finish, just picked up a clod of dirt.

Then, as the older horses swayed into their collars and began the start, he threw it at Brownie as the horse stood there merely looking up contentedly toward his master.

The clod struck Brownie on the flank. He winced and jumped.

"You, hey . . . you stop throwing clods . . . you . . . Brownie, get up, boy. Get into it."

Brownie struck his weight into his collar with a lurch. All the others, heads down and backs humping and quarters wrinkling, had been giving a long lift to roll the wheels out of the standing ruts they had made in the soft ground. This extra fillip was all that was needed, and it seemed that Brownie's effort alone made the wagons lurch forward.

On the road beside the house, Tommy Grant climbed down from his driving seat, gave Brownie a casual pat, and walked into the kitchen.

"Here's the list," said Margie.

"All right."

He took it, and went stalking on through the dining room, up the creaking stairs to the attic.

He had no purpose in going there, but he was blind with rage because Brownie had been stoned by Train, because that rascal would again refuse to pay the back wages, because, well, most of all because he felt his own childish impotence in dealing with the rancher. In his wrath, he saw at once the holstered Winchester that hung from two nails just over his cot, with the Colt beside it. He took the Colt down and slung it so that it was under his left arm. Then he put on the jumper coat of his overalls. It had not been used much, and the stiff cloth concealed the gun perfectly.

He could not tell why he had put on the gun, but he knew that the weight of it dragging at his shoulders, and the bulk of it under his arm, made him feel better. The sense of tragedy and tragic helplessness disappeared, and began to seem no more than the morning blues. So he kept the gun on as he walked down the stairs and into the kitchen.

Margie turned around at the sink. There was a dark splotch of wet across her apron where the dish water had splashed, and as she opened her eyes at him, she looked like a child.

"What's the matter, Tommy?" she asked.

He paused in the doorway and began to make a cigarette.

"There's too much Tommy. That's what's the matter," he said. "Too much Tommy, and not enough man."

"Are you angry? Are you really angry?"

"No. Not much. I'm used to it . . . being kicked around."

"What in the world is under your jumper?"

She came across the kitchen, pointing. He caught her wrist, hard, before she could touch him, and the wreckage of the cigarette floated to the floor in a little yellow cloud. She had not paid the slightest attention when he said that he was used to being kicked around. Even if she despised him, she need not show it so openly.

"Tommy, what is under that coat?"

"Never mind!"

She grew white.

"What is it? What are you going to do?"

"Nothing. Never mind."

Her distress gave him a savage and melancholy triumph. She had guessed that it was a weapon, and apparently she credited him with the will to use it. More credit than he deserved, perhaps, but nevertheless his vanity was fed. She was afraid. That showed that she believed in him, a little.

He released her hand. She stepped closer, and held up her face. It amazed him, but if this was the way of it, he must take her in his arms, strongly, and kiss her. As a matter of fact, what he wanted to do was to sit down and ask a great many questions until he grew used to the new idea. However, custom must be served. He put his arms about her and kissed her. Then he saw a horror in her face, and felt the gun pressed against him by her body.

"It's a revolver!" she said.

"Well, never mind." He stepped back hastily. He was about to tell her that there was no meaning behind all this—that it was no more than a childish gesture. But now that he had crossed the mysterious threshold and passed into her being, and she into his, he must make no more childish gestures. He wanted to ask her if she really meant it. If she really could love him. If she had cared about him long. But that did not seem to be the thing to do. Her calm attitude of acceptance made everything a matter of course. Would other men envy him, or would they laugh? She was not so very pretty, except for her hair and the green eyes and a sort of glow that was about her. She was small, too. A lot of people would think it ridiculous if he married such a small girl.

I am a fake. I am a sham, he thought. Even at this instant when his heart should have been rioting with joy, he was analyzing and criticizing like the cold soul and cruel, empty nature that was really his. And now a great resolve was born in him. He was nothing, he was a mere worthless, floating leaf in the current of human events, but now that he had a woman, he would have to make her look up to him. His life must become, from this moment, devoted to a colossal deception, and no matter how his heart quaked in him, he must appear to her to stand four-square to all the winds.

"It's a revolver! You've got a revolver there under your coat! Is it loaded, Tommy? What are you going to do with it?"

"Never mind. Nothing."

"I've got a right to know!"

Electric pricklings ran from his forehead straight back into his brain. She had a right to know!

Then he made himself frown at her. "You've got a right to know . . . someday you will know. So long, Margie."

Up his spine ran a chilly fear that she might run after him to the door. He opened it with haste and stepped outside, but when he glanced back, in closing it, he saw that she had not moved from her place in the middle of the floor, and that her face was still white.

He had to do something. He simply couldn't come back to the house without doing something.

Sylvester Train began to give orders as soon as he saw his hired hand coming from the house.

"Get them rolling and keep them rolling, Tommy," he directed. "And mind the railroad crossing. That Swede who works for Milligan let the wagon get away from him on that grade, the other day. Whole thing dumped into the ditch. When you get the check from the warehouse, take it to the bank. Deposit it all but forty dollars . . ."

"About money," said the boy.

Train raised his hand.

"Buy the things on the list, and then take ten dollars for yourself and give yourself a little party. You stay pretty close to your job. You're a good, faithful lad, Tommy. And all work and no play makes Tommy a dull boy, eh?"

He smiled, almost tenderly, on Tommy Grant, and the iron went out of the boy's resolution.

Still he persisted: "You know, about money . . . I've been thinking that I'd like to have the back months of wages."

"Of course you'll have them, whenever you want them."

"Well, I'd like to have them today, then. If . . ."

"Wait a minute," said Train. "How many months of back pay do I owe to you? Six or seven?"

"Six or seven! Nineteen months, all told."

"Nineteen?"

"Yes. I have the account. You can't . . ."

"I can't what? The point is . . . I don't dispute your account in the slightest . . . but the point is that you are dropping on me for all that money on the spur of the moment."

"Well . . . ," began Tommy Grant.

"I don't believe it," muttered Sylvester Train. "Not an open-hearted, honest lad like you,

Tommy. You wouldn't try to put on sudden pressure. You wouldn't try to injure me. No, not after four years, when you've lived in my house like a son. You wouldn't have malice. Not after eating bread and meat at my table. Nothing will convince me that he has malice in him."

He shook his head, regarding Tommy Grant sorrowfully.

Shame came upon Tommy.

"Look, Mister Train," he said. "I don't want to injure you. Of course pay for a year and a half is a good deal. I'd forgotten about that. I don't want to be mean about it."

"If you want your money, you shall have it. That's flat. I simply want a day or two to get things in readiness. You give me a shock, Tommy. It's as though you've decided to leave me. To leave this house. Your home! I can't believe it. Perhaps because I sometimes speak sharply? Ah, well, as John A. Creevy used to say . . . 'Paternal affection has a stern voice.' As on a son I look on you. Mine is a childless life, Tommy. God knows that I have no right to you . . . no claim upon you. But the heart will speak out, like a tyrant. I have spoken too freely. You are revolted. You say to yourself that the old man is in his dotage. It's true that I'm old. . . ."

"No, Mister Train . . . I only meant . . ."

"I'm old," said Sylvester Train huskily. "My days are limited. I know it. I don't complain. The

147

endings of things are as their beginning. A lonely life shall reap a lonely death."

"About the money . . . there's no hurry," said Tommy Grant. He was moved, and his voice was unsteady.

"No, you shall have it. Every penny. If I have to go to the poorhouse, you shall have every penny."

"I don't want to inconvenience or injure you. I really don't."

"Ah, my lad, youth is thoughtless. The swift mind of youth is careless. And the heel of youth wears a spur that is often buried, I fear, in the hearts of those who love them. I won't say any more about that. I'm sorry that you've moved me so, Tommy. I'm not often stirred, like this. But where a man's heart is enlisted, his judgment and his will are weak. Well . . . I'm sorry to make a show of myself. You shall have every penny."

"I don't want it!" cried out Tommy Grant. "Great Scott . . . I don't want it. I only thought . . ."

"You don't want it? Well, after all, why should you be worried? I should not worry, if I were you. I'm old, Tommy, and not as strong as I once was. The sleepless nights . . . they mean something. The growing weakness . . . I don't talk about such things, but I'm not blind. Still, in the end, I must leave my land to someone. To whom, then? Did you ever think of that? Well, *I* have thought of it, Tommy. Now go to town and take the ten dollars, and have a good, carefree time. *You* can. Life is still a small burden to you. Go on, my lad! Your heart is light. As for the hearts of old men, they don't matter."

IV

There were tears in the eyes of Tommy Grant, as he started the team down the road. He was halfway to the town of Fruit Dale before he began to wonder if it had not been a trick, after all—another trick from the inexhaustible store of Sylvester Train, putting off the day of payment from time to time until, perhaps, it would never come. So, again, he had won in the matter of the brown colt. If Brownie could not be worked in the plow team, at least, he could be used on the road—and therefore the road work began. All that belonged to Sylvester Train was carefully arranged so that nothing should be wasted. Land, friendship, money, horses, relations— all were worked into the careful pattern of his schemes.

How much money did the old man have? He never lost in his ventures, he never wasted his dollars in friendly loans. He lived on next to nothing. Surely there must be a certain amount of fat in the bank account of this fellow who pretended that even to pay his hired laborer, his farm hand, was too great a strain.

Anger gathered like clouds in the mind of Tommy, but he realized mournfully that anger had gathered in him many times before on the same subject, though it never had given him a cutting edge when it came to dealing with the tyrant.

They came into Fruit Dale past the wretched little gnarled apple orchard which had given the town its name, so many years ago. He swung the team in a wide arc across the street before the warehouse, and stopped as the shadow of the place swept over them. Brownie was dancing as Sid Levine walked over to the entrance.

"Hey, Tommy! Looks like quite a load you got there," Levine said with a smirk. "Best get this unloaded." He called out to a couple of his men to give Tommy a hand.

Tommy Grant remained silent, never really having liked Levine and his propensity for gossip. He hoisted a couple of the bags and looked at Levine for instructions as to where he was to put them.

"Over there . . . on the right," the warehouse manager told him as he stood there watching Tommy. Luckily, two of his assistants showed up just then.

"Have you seen Bert Ellis, Tommy?" Levine asked as Tommy walked past him on the way back to pick up another load.

Tommy just shook his head.

"Heard that Lefty Lew Hilton is looking for

him," Levine said, oblivious to the fact that Tommy was ignoring his questions. "Ready to take him on, Hilton is. Says he ain't got no use for that murderer Ellis, I've heard. You went to school with Ellis, didn't you, Tommy?"

Tommy nodded his head, becoming more agitated with Levine's unending flurry of questions. He was just about ready to tell him to shut up when Levine was called to the back of the warehouse.

In fifteen minutes' time the trio of men had the wagons unloaded. So all Tommy had to do now was wait for Levine to come out with the payment. He stood in the doorway watching the comings and goings of the townsfolk, most of whom he only knew by sight.

Then like thunder on his mind, the voice of Sid Levine could be heard coming up behind him.

"That's a girl you got out there, ain't it?"

"What?" Tommy Grant shot back.

"You don't know. You don't know why you stay on with that fat swine of a Train. You don't know nothing about it, I guess not."

Sid Levine was laughing. He broke off to shout: "I'd work for nothing, too, to look at her three times a day. She's class, is what she is."

The boy smiled rather sickly. Of course he should be above desirous assurance and especially from such a one as Sid Levine, and yet he knew that he was relieved. Not much of a man. That was the trouble with him. He was not much of a man!

Levine handed him the check once he was assured the two wagons were stripped of their load.

Tommy looked at the bare boards of the wagons, polished by much friction, shimmering in the sunlight. A hundred sacks of grain—that would feed a whole town for a day. He felt a sense of dignity as he climbed up on the wagon and pulled on the jerk-line to rouse Bird.

He shouted: "Get up! Ye-ay, boys!"

The whole team leaned forward, the wagons started, and rumbled out of the great warehouse into the blinding heat and dazzle of the sun.

The team shocked along at an easy trot until he reached the big trees along Washington Street, and there at the tying racks he tethered them to wait while he went about his tasks. The check was for the bank, with ten of it for himself. Ten dollars, on account of nineteen months of back pay!

Well, Sid Levine was a fellow who had been in the Navy. He had seen the world. He had said that *he* would be willing to work for nothing . . . if he could see Margie every day!

But why should he have to borrow assurance from anyone? That was the trouble.

After he went to the bank, he did the shopping. He bought six pairs of the rubber gloves for

Margie and paid for them out of his ten dollars. He was heading back for Washington Street and the team, when he met Bert Ellis, and Ellis actually stopped to speak to him.

He was a handsome fellow, that Ellis. He flashed in the sunlight in his suit of linen. He wore white canvas shoes with fancy tops of yellow leather. He had a blue-bordered handkerchief sticking out of a breast pocket. He looked cool in the furnace of that early afternoon. There was a walking stick in his hand. Not two men in Fruit Dale, outside of Bert Ellis, would have dared to descend to this itemized dandyism, or to flaunt it in the face of the public. But Bert Ellis was Bert Ellis. It was not for *one* killing that he had been sent to prison. The only mystery was that he had not been hanged—few who had done far less had escaped with a term so short. But after all, they had little damning proof that was more than circumstantial, and how could a jury, how could a judge look into the young face and the big, brown, steady eyes of Bert Ellis without granting him a certain modicum of trust.

"I'll tell you something about yourself, Tommy," he said, leaning a little on his walking stick and making it bend, as he spoke. "What I mean is . . . you need a drink and I'm going to buy it."

He picked half of the parcels out of the arms of Tommy, and carried them. He kicked open

155

the doors of the saloon, and put his burden down carefully on a chair. Then he stood at the bar with Tommy Grant, and, taking off his hat, Ellis was removing the perspiration from his forehead with a handkerchief, not giving it a hearty swipe like a man, but dabbing like a woman who has make-up that may be blurred. He touched his upper lip, and the beads of perspiration no longer glimmered there. He was very dainty. He was very delicate.

"Here's my idea," Ellis said.

Eyewitnesses had seen him lift nine hundred and seventeen pounds of iron junk onto a scale, but no one guessed it to look at him, unless one took careful note of the depth of his chest and the way his collar sat up on the slope of his neck.

"Beer sounds good to me," said Tommy. He laughed a little. He never had dreamed that Bert Ellis would pay any attention to him, to pick him up in the street like this.

The beer came. Bert Ellis paid for it with a five-dollar bill which he creased with deft fingers so that it stood out straight as a card when he offered it. When he took up his change with one gesture, he made the silver disappear into one pocket, the bills into another.

Imagine what a man like that would be with a gun!

They drank. The beer was very cold. The first swallow sent a numb pang toward the brain of

Tommy. Ice cream does the same thing. Peace descended upon Tommy Grant, calm content poured up from a fountain that was near his heart.

"You know, Bert, I was going to tell you something. Here, bartender. We'll have another beer."

Bert Ellis laid on his wrist a finger as cool and as heavy as steel.

"*You* have another, if you want, Tommy. One will do for me."

"Let me buy you a drink, Bert, will you?"

"You save your money, Tommy. You don't get much from that man Train, I suppose."

His glance slipped over the clothes of Tommy Grant. It was a mere flick of the eye, and Tommy pretended not to notice, yet he had seen and felt the thing.

It was cool in the saloon. You would hardly imagine that the autumn day was white-hot outside. The window was set with green panes and red that gleamed like jewels. Imagine what it would cost to buy emeralds and rubies as big as that!

"I won't drink alone," Tommy insisted.

"Well, I'll take a small one. Two more, Joe."

One could feel that Bert Ellis knew many bartenders by their first names.

"All right, Mister Ellis. This beer is cold enough, ain't it?" Joe asked with hesitation.

"Yeah. They have it colder at The Paradise,

though, Joe. It freezes your teeth, down there."
He turned his attention back to Tommy. "You
were going to tell me something. . . ."

The door to the back room of the saloon opened,
and three men came out silently. They huddled
shoulder to shoulder through the swinging doors
and went out with their heads lowered, as though
into a pouring rain.

"What's the matter with them, Joe?" Bert Ellis
asked the bartender.

"Roulette. They've been bucking it all afternoon . . . poor devils."

"Roulette's the devil," Bert Ellis stated.

"I was just going to tell you, Bert . . . ," Tommy
Grant began again, "maybe it doesn't mean a
thing, but I was just going to tell you anyway.
I was down the street, and I heard somebody
mention you."

"Who?"

"I won't tell you that. But this person said that
Lefty Lew Hilton was going around town looking
for you."

"Lefty? Oh."

Ellis looked calmly over his shoulder toward
the door. There was no one coming in or going
out. Tommy Grant knew that if there was a man
on the range, Lefty Lew was the one to match this
dark-skinned man-slayer at any sort of a game.

Tommy looked over the line of bottles that
stood in front of the mirror, each with its brighter

image floating in the glass behind. There are men in this world who shine like that—Bert Ellis was one of them, in his linen suit, with the big diamond stuck in his necktie. There were others who are always drab—like Tommy Grant.

"I just thought you might want to know. That's all. Maybe there's nothing in it."

"If Lefty wants me, I hope he doesn't have to hunt too long. I'm not living in a hole in the ground."

"No, of course not," Tommy agreed.

Bert Ellis moved a little, so that his left elbow touched the bar, resting lightly upon it. In this position he commanded the swinging door, the window, the door into the gambling room. Also, his right hand was free for instant action.

A lump of excitement began to rise in the throat of Tommy. He had to do something before he went back to Margie. But perhaps it would be enough if he simply saw something at first-hand—something important.

"By the way, Tommy."

"Yes?"

"How are things out there at the Train place?"

"Pretty good."

"How good is that?"

"Oh, just pretty good."

"Margie's the pretty part of it, eh?"

Tommy looked hard and sharp at the other. Sid Levine had spoken of her almost at once. Now a

159

second man was saying the same type of things. Perhaps Bert Ellis had brought him into the saloon only to talk of the girl.

"Margie's all right," Tommy said slowly.

"Of course she is. Only, the other night at the dance, I asked her to step around with me three times. She only accepted once. She was with you. The other two times, she sat them out."

Tommy rolled his eyes before saying: "You know, Bert. Girls are funny about things. They don't mean anything. They're just funny."

"Does she think that I'm a blight . . . or something?"

"Oh, no. I'm sure she didn't. She's just sort of funny. That's all. Girls are sort of funny about things. You never know."

"Did she say anything about me, afterward?"

"Margie? Why, no."

"Not a word?"

"You know . . . something about the way you danced. She says you're a wonderful dancer."

"Too wonderful, eh? Make her conspicuous, or something?"

"No. I don't think that's what she meant."

He felt the brown, probing eyes of the other rest on him with critical insight.

When he couldn't take it any longer, he broke out: "Bert, what are you driving at? Are you interested in Margie? She's not pretty enough to interest you, Bert."

Bert smiled in an odd way.

"Pretty? She's not so pretty, but she's interesting enough. Enough to keep me awake at night. Give me a whiskey, Joe."

"Lefty's looking for you," suggested the boy. "You don't want whiskey, do you?"

Ellis handled the glass and the bottle that had been placed in front of him. He filled the glass half full and pushed it toward the bartender. "You drink this for me, Joe."

He faced back at Tommy Grant to say: "Now, brother, you tell me something."

"What?"

"You were always head of the class when we were in school. I want you to recite for me. I'm not joking," he added as Tommy frowned. "The way you did history . . . that was pretty good."

"It didn't lead to anything. There's nothing practical about history."

He could see the pages of the books. He could hear his own voice rising in the classroom, while the teacher listened with eyes askance, rather bored to have to hear words that repeated the book so closely. Well, in those days he could remember that everyone had expected him to go on and do something with his brain—to be a lawyer, or something like that. In those days, he had respected himself.

"You're not practical. No," Bert Ellis said, nodding his head. "But *I* am. I've done things that practically hanged me. That's being practical, all right."

Still he was smiling, as he said this, but men were almost always smiling when they talked to Tommy Grant. Men nearly always spoke to him with a certain reservation, as though they would remember his words in order to laugh at them later on.

"You've done things," said Tommy Grant. "You've been around, and you've done things."

"Not the things that a girl like Margie cares about," Bert Ellis said, and he laid his right hand flat on the bar and turned his back on the doors and window while he stared at Tommy Grant. And outside, somewhere, was Lew Hilton, with the soul of a hungry bobcat. "You have a brain . . . so now you tell me about Margie, will you?"

His earnestness acted almost hypnotically on Tommy, and the latter, half squinting his eyes, felt the bar room dissolve before him, and in its place came the picture of the open countryside, with the mountains in the distance and the black soil glinting from the rains, and the house of Sylvester Train set in the middle of the universe, as it were, with Margie in the kitchen, washing dishes, a black, wet mark across the front of her apron.

He said: "I see it this way . . . what a man has in his head, he can do with his hands . . . but what a woman does with her hands doesn't matter. You can tell a man by what he does . . . you can't tell a woman. Margie knows me, but I don't know Margie. She knows me by what I say . . . I can only guess at her by what she doesn't say. When she's happy, I pity her because she's glad. When she's sad, I smile a little, as though she weren't old enough to know what trouble really is. I don't know anything about her, and that's why I'm close to her."

"I asked for this," Bert Ellis said grimly, "and . . . well are you close to her?"

"Yes. But I don't know why."

"Does she?"

"Yes, but she couldn't say why . . . in words."

"You were always like this . . . always different from the rest of us," said Ellis gloomily. "You make me feel like a little kid. I don't know anything. I'm back in school and don't know anything, when you talk. Aw, well . . . let's go in there where we can sit down. I want to talk some more. Let's go in there and play a game of cards."

"I've only got seven, eight dollars."

"We'll play light. I don't care about your money. I want to talk."

They went into the back room. It had three windows. Two of them were shuttered against the heat. The one that was open let in a slanting stream of light that rushed through the motes of dust and smoke like water down a flume. It made the roulette wheel a flash of fire. It penciled the legs of the card tables with long, straight highlights. There were only half a dozen men in there. It was the dull time of the day.

"I ought to be starting back home," said Tommy Grant. For he was afraid, when he saw this room, and the careless, confident faces of the men. They all seemed to be risking their money with a kingly indifference, killing time, and waiting for something of importance to happen.

"You stay a while," insisted Bert Ellis. "I want to talk some more. I haven't seen you for a long time, and I wanna talk some more. Stud?"

"How about seven-up? I wouldn't know how to play stud poker. That's pretty fast . . . when you've only got a few dollars in your pocket."

"All right. Seven-up it is," said Bert Ellis. He smiled.

The heart of Tommy Grant turned into a small lump of lead. He felt a feeble anger against Train. If he had received his back pay, at least he would be able to play cards like a man.

V

He made up his mind that he would play boldly, lose his few dollars with speed, and then finish the talk with Bert Ellis. Bert wanted to know about Margie. Bert liked Margie. He said that she was more than pretty. And Margie had kissed him good bye. She had not said one word of love, but she had kissed Tommy Grant good bye, as though everything were understood.

His mind was full of this and not of the game. Seven-up is a simple game. There are four possible points in a hand—high, low, Jack of the trump suit, and game, which goes with the play of the cards. If you want to bid all four at once, you "shoot the moon." If you win, the game is yours. If you lose, you're set far back. The game is what you decide on at the time—eleven points, perhaps. They played for quarters, fifty cents, dollars. Bert Ellis was as one whose thoughts are otherwhere, on words he was about to speak.

Tommy Grant, waiting for those words to be spoken, found that an hour had gone by and that he had forty dollars. That was a lot of money. It gave him a sense of power and a sense of guilt.

He leaned forward and pulled in fresh winnings. The gun under his jacket rapped the edge of the table, and suddenly Bert Ellis cocked a forefinger at him. The dreaminess was gone.

"You're packing something under your coat!" he exclaimed.

Tommy had his feet resting on the round rung that encircled the legs of the table. At this sudden remark, he dropped his feet to the floor with a bump. It seemed to him that everybody in the room was staring at him, but then he realized that the words had been spoken softly.

"I brought a gun in with me," Tommy Grant admitted. "Rabbits along the road, sometimes. . . ."

The face of Ellis was grave, but his eyes glittered.

"You want to know how to use a gun before you wear one. Who steered you to wear a gun?"

"I don't know."

"That's all right," said Bert Ellis. "You've got a gun, and that's all right. Here, Judge! Come here!"

Bert Ellis tilted his chair back. The whole atmosphere had altered. It was as though the great Bert Ellis were angered because he had lost forty dollars! Tommy felt that he was enclosed in a mystery as in a dream. He wanted to escape from the nightmare into the open day. His nerves were jumping with fear, but he remembered that one cannot leave a game while one is a winner. He was half of a mind to push the money across the table and then leave.

Although he had nothing to do with the law—

except for being on the wrong side of it—Judge Carson came across the room. He wore a long black coat, buttoned tight about the breast. He had a pair of old-fashioned saber-shaped mustaches and a short, pointed beard. On the edge of the table he rested the tips of his fingers, and those fingers were as slender and round as pencils, and the color of ivory.

"Judge, give me a hundred dollars," Bert Ellis said.

Carson took out a roll of bills, which he passed without counting them. They were accepted in the same spirit. Judge Carson had been looking at Tommy Grant all the while, then turned before he was thanked and crossed the room to his former place.

"Now to start again," said Bert Ellis.

"What's the matter, Bert?" Tommy asked in alarm.

"Nothing's the matter. We've got a good little game going here. That's all. Later on, I wanna talk some more about Margie. I can understand what she sees in you, now. It's because of the queer lingo you can throw . . . and because you're old enough to wear a gun."

His lips twitched to the side as though he felt nausea.

"Well, I couldn't learn that lingo . . . all that history, arithmetic, science . . . that book stuff," concluded Bert Ellis. "Go on! It's your deal!"

He pushed over the cards, flashing his glance up and down the person of Tommy Grant. It seemed clear to the boy that what angered Ellis was not the loss of money, but the escape of Margie from his device or his hope, whatever it had been.

At any rate, there was a devil in Ellis, now. The other men left the room. And through the open door, Tommy Grant could see Judge Carson watching him from his table. The man shook his head, then laughed in a tone that jarred through all the nerves of Tommy Grant even from across the other room. He wanted to leap up and rush from Ellis and the man trap Tommy felt he was setting, but something compelled him to stay there. He might have explained it by saying that he wished to find out exactly what devil was working in Ellis, and how its manifestation might effect Margie. Or was it only an imp of the perverse that chained him there with a nightmare weakness.

"When's the marriage date?" snarled Ellis.

"What marriage?"

"He asked me 'what marriage?' That's good. Well . . . all right."

Ellis dealt out the cards.

Now, suddenly, Ellis began to win. He was betting on the side, and Tommy accepted those bets with a dumb submission. It was better to lose money than blood, he vaguely felt.

At least one thing was learned, never to be forgotten—that it is better for sheep to keep with sheep, and wolves with wolves. Now and again, Bert rubbed his hands together, washing them in the air, wringing the fingers hard together as though to keep up the circulation.

Someone came in and unshuttered the two other windows. The sunlight sloped in at a different angle. It was golden in color, and the day was growing old. Tommy Grant had only a fleeting thought of the team waiting down there on Washington Street, under the trees, with the long road home before them. It would be long after dark when they would finally arrive at Sylvester Train's ranch. The bay mare would be whinnying from loneliness in the barn.

But their driver sat in the back room of a saloon, entangled in a strange destiny. He felt the cold breath of it on his face—no, that was the force of the electric fan, which hummed and sang in a corner, sending its wavering current from side to side, as it oscillated. The sound it made reminded him of many voices in the distance—women all talking together in excitement.

He had ten dollars left of the forty—less than that. The thing would be over soon. And then he saw—no, he did not really see. It was merely a gleam that issued from the cuff of Ellis's right sleeve. But that half guessed at gleam suddenly struck a darkness through the brain of Tommy Grant.

"Just a minute," he said, and, reaching out, he swept the cards together.

"What's the idea. What's the general idea of gumming up my deal?" asked Ellis sharply.

Tommy flicked the cards out rapidly.

"There's only fifty cards on the table," he said. "Where's the other two?"

He looked up from his counting. He felt that it was safe for him to be angry, because Bert Ellis was a famous warrior, a man of guns. He would never use guns on an old friend, an inexperienced simple fellow like himself. Then he saw he was wrong.

Ellis was leaning forward a little, resting his left hand on the edge of the table. Around his smiling lips there was whiteness.

Tommy watched Ellis's right hand flick beneath the table. Two cards rose in a glistening arc and dropped on the rest.

"There's fifty-two now," said Ellis. "What about it?"

"My God, Bert!" Tommy gasped.

"What about it?" asked Ellis. "What about it, and what about the marriage? I'm ready for the rest of that talk . . . it'll be short."

His right shoulder twitched.

He's going to kill me! said the brain of Tommy.

He stiffened. His feet were resting on the rung

of the table again, and as his muscles jumped, the table edge was driven back against Ellis, knocking his right arm to the side as he raised it and the shining gun that his hand grasped.

Tommy had spilled sidewise from his chair. He was on his knees. He own gun was out, shuddering, making his whole arm shake from the wrist to the shoulder.

"You fool, put up . . . ," began Bert Ellis.

That was all. For a shadow rose up outside the open window on the left, and a gun spoke. Bert Ellis fired not at Tommy Grant, but with instant change of aim toward the open window. The sound of the first shot made the trigger finger of Tommy contract, and the roar of his own Colt deafened him as a bullet went into the floor.

He stood up. The shadow was gone from the window. Bert Ellis was on his knees, gripping the edge of the table with both hands.

"Whatcha think of that?" he whispered. "Now, whatcha think of that?"

His lips twisted into a knot, all on one side. He got to his feet, made two short steps toward the windows, and fell flat on his back. His head bounced as it hit the floor. The revolver skidded to the farther corner, collided with the wall, and exploded again.

Tommy leaned above the dead man. The dead eyes looked straight back at him with a distinct message. The mouth was still drawn into a loose knot, all on one side, half agony and half a sneer.

Then twenty people were in the room. They glided about, making no noise, muttering to one another. Doc Purvis, the sheriff, stood beside Judge Carson. The humped shoulders of Purvis and the old felt hat which he wore pushed back on his stiff, gray thatch of hair had always meant to Tommy the reassuring might of the law, which keeps the weak from harm, but they had another meaning now.

"He fired from outside that window!" cried Tommy. "He can't be far away . . . he . . ."

All the men who had been looking at the dead body turned toward Tommy, as though surprised to hear his voice.

"That's all right," said Sheriff Purvis. "Give me your gun."

He reached out his hand for the weapon, but his head was already turned back toward Carson.

The latter was saying calmly, as one who speaks of an event that had happened years before: "They were playing cards at that table. They were playing seven-up. The kid had won some money. Bert asked me for a stake. I gave him a hundred bucks. I went out into the bar and had a drink. It was funny . . . Bert losing money to a kid like that. We were all laughing. There's where Bert was sitting. You see where the coins is stacked, now. That means he was winning everything back. It guess it looked like a lot of money to the kid. He'd been drinking. I guess he thought he was rich, so he started a gunplay. I guess he took Bert by surprise. Winning a few bucks, I guess the kid thought he was rich, and he didn't want to lose it again."

"Lew Hilton'll be glad to hear about this," someone said.

"All right, boy," said the sheriff, and he half turned to Tommy again.

They were all so calm. That was what made it more of a nightmare, more of the same nightmare that had been holding Tommy Grant from the moment he had entered this horrible room. They would hang him in the same way—casually. The hangman would talk to his assistant of other things, while carelessly knotting the rope about Tommy's neck. People would look at his death struggles as they might stare at a fish snapping and jerking on the end of a line.

It was all a nightmare, but you can die in a dream like that! And there was the door to the bar room, not three steps away.

Tommy Grant covered those three steps in one bound, catching the edge of the door as he shot by, and wrenching it shut behind him. The door split from the top half all the way to the bottom with a little round hole bored in the center of the crack. Someone had fired after him.

In the first hundredth part of a second, he noted those details and wondered why he had not heard the gun explode. In the next wink of time, he had turned the key in the lock. A torrent of noise of feet and shoutings roared across the inner room, crashed against the door, battered, and shook it. It sagged top and bottom, but the bolt of the lock held.

Tommy Grant ran through the saloon to the street, right past the white face of Joe. He had seemed a formidable fellow who worked behind a bar merely so that he might observe more closely the follies of lesser men, but now his face was white stone. He was brittle. A touch would break him.

Tommy ran straight across the street, turned down to the next corner, rounded that corner, and gathered headway down a by-lane as the uproar of the pursuit came out of the saloon behind him.

The noise was something like that of a spoken word that begins with a deep humming in the throat, reaches the lips, parts them of its own force, and then shouts upon the ear. So that clamor of the pursuit issued from the swinging doors of the saloon.

They will kill me . . . they will shoot me through the back! was the only thought running through Tommy's head.

People on the street before him yelled, dodged here and there into doorways. A woman stumbled and fell in the dust of the street. She lay there helpless, kicking, screeching for help.

Then Tommy realized that the naked revolver was still in his hand. He shoved it back into the holster, still running at full speed. When you run with all your might, there is a certain smoothness about the action, like the difference between sitting a horse that gallops, and a horse that is racing. So Tommy Grant, as he sprinted for his life, felt that his brain was clear and steady. It was like being swept down a flume toward a waterfall, and not caring about the drop that is swiftly to come.

He wondered if they would catch him before he got to Washington Street, but, as a matter of fact, the sounds were mixed and far behind him. Then he saw the team ahead, and ran harder than ever, for he realized for the first time why he had gone for the team instead of taking the first saddled horse that he saw. It was Brownie. He had to have the colt between his knees, and the insanity of this world would straighten out, somehow.

As he ran the last few steps, he pulled out his clasp knife, opened the middle blade, and in three slashes he had the colt out of harness.

He looked back. Across the street several people were staring at him—but the head of the pursuit that roared in the distance had not yet come in sight. So he tore the rest of the harness from the back of Brownie and jumped on his back. There was only the collar remaining. He unbuckled that as he sat in place, and let it fall into the dust. There was no bridle, only the halter and tie rope, but he could guide Brownie perfectly with no better equipment than this.

The big gelding stepped out, flirted its tail, and then swung into a long, easy canter. Now Tommy Grant looked back again, and as he did so, he saw three riders round the corner two blocks behind him. They came around like racers, swinging their quirts, their horses slanting in at a sharp angle, then they straightened and came for him with all their might.

VI

A good horse can sprint for a mile. After that, it begins to go in the wind, then in the knees. Also, a sudden start kills off a horse. It needs to be warmed up. Tommy Grant knew about that, and he eased the brown colt down the road toward Comanche Pass at a three-quarter pace, well inside his full strength. The road was only a gentle slope, and Brownie could use his long legs to the fullest advantage. Fifty riders composed the long train that swept out of Fruit Dale in the pursuit. Through the dust and the confusion, Tommy could see the first leaders falling back, and others come up in their places. That was at the end of the second mile. At the end of the third, they began to shoot. One bullet sang a note at his ear that remained in his mind the rest of his life; the rest came nowhere near. Those fellows were shooting because they were beginning to lose the race. The whole lot of them fell gradually back.

It was five miles to the point where the graded road disappeared at a triple branching of the way. One turned to the right, one to the left, and the middle one went straight on for Comanche Pass.

It was a loosely winding trail, and Tommy took the colt across country to follow something closer to the flight of a bird, for the best thing that

Brownie did was to jump. The fences were low barbed wire, but Brownie knew all about barbed wire. He hopped across a dozen of these fences and before he had passed into the open range land of the upper hills, right under Comanche Pass, there was not a sight or a sound of all that strong river of men which had issued from Fruit Dale for the manhunt.

Some of them, and those the better part, were back there struggling across the open country and the rest either had returned to the town or else were following along the easier windings of the trail that led toward the Pass. As though he would be fool enough to attempt to go straight through the Pass! Those fellows who came straight behind would have to stop to cut the wires of a dozen fences and that took a little time, even with the best of snippers. At any rate they were well behind before Tommy Grant veered a little to the left and rode into the trees.

The moment he was among them he felt better. The ride had been one long glory for the brown colt. Now he began to taste some glory for himself as the sunset fire ran up the faces of the cliffs, and the sweetness of the pines filled the air. The moment and the place seemed made for him, and when he looked into the future, for the first time in his mature life, he appeared secure against the sneers and the scorns of his fellows. You don't sneer at a man who is supposed to have killed another in a gunfight. You may vote prison for him, but you don't sneer.

What would Margie say about it? Would Sylvester Train feel, now, that perhaps he might never have to pay those months of arrears in pay? And what would he do with himself tonight? What would he do with himself in all the nights that were to come—before the wave of the law overtook him and bore him down into the long darkness?

He rode from the darkness of the trees up the side of an isolated crag. It stood in the forest like the prow of a ship in the sea, and looking down through the blaze of golden light, through the long, cool shadows beneath him, he saw a dust cloud rolling slowly uphill, and in the cloud he counted seven forms. They might be seeing him far more easily than he could see them, but, nevertheless, he lingered to watch them. Seven out of fifty!

Sometime in the future perhaps a gray-haired man would sit by the fire of a winter night and tell his children how the riding had gone, on the day when Tom Grant killed the gunman, Bert Ellis. How the fifty had dwindled. How only seven remained to climb the steep eastern ramparts near Comanche Pass. They would have to speak of the brown colt, when they spoke of this ride, and they would have to speak of him as well.

All sleek and bright with sweat, Brownie shone

beneath him and lifted his fine head, and pricked his ears at the sunset. Intolerable joy swelled the heart of Tommy until it ached.

He rode back from the edge of the crag and entered the forest again. The shadows hardly bothered him, because he knew this ground as only a hunter could know it. When he had a day off, he used to rise at three in the morning, take the old Winchester from its holster, and ride up here to hunt. He could recognize individual trees, stumps, rivulets that trickled across the way, still icy from the snows that were melting above timberline.

He came to a clearing, and looked down from the steep slope to Fruit Dale, that seemed sheer beneath. It was a little toy that one could pick up in the hand, and now lights were coming on, sending up delicate rays through the evening darkness. Yonder in the west, the sun was out of sight, but it was not yet down, and all the western mountains were painted with black, thick oil paint on a sheet of flame.

He entered the forest again, dismounted, and began to climb up a slope at an angle of fifty-five degrees, slipping back often on the uneasy surface of the pine needles. He knew just where to be by the time the darkness had gathered.

He found the place where running water had worn away the upper soil until the roots of the trees were exposed, along with the brown bones of the mountain beneath the skin. Up that natural trench he climbed. Sometimes he had to pause to encourage Brownie with a word. Twice he slipped up to the knee in the white rush of water. It sounded loud above him and below, but it was no more than a hushing noise, like wind, immediately beneath him. When he had struggled to a distance up that uncomfortable ladder, he turned aside up a dry draw, turned again through dense woods, and came out on a little shoulder of land where a cabin was backed against the head of the mountain.

From here, he looked out across the world. The western heights were less than half their former height. Their roots seemed to be dissolving in darkness, like sand in water. They had settled down, and behind them the sunset was a dirty smudge. The wind was from the east. When it puffed down the slope above him, it ran over his body like water. Then how did it feel on the wet hide of Brownie?

There was good grazing on the mountain shoulder.

About the edges of the cabin the grass grew longer. The dead, brown growth of the last season was still standing there. So he tore up a quantity of this, twisted it into hard wisps, and dressed the colt thoroughly, rubbing and rubbing until the wet was gone. Rubbing until the dampness disappeared and Brownie was dry from his sensitive face down the sleekness of that strong body, to the hammered iron of his legs.

Then he went into the cabin and lighted a match. Everything was exactly as he had left it. The pile of pine branches of which he had made his bed was turning brown—that was the only difference. The old axe, its head brown with rust, leaned in the corner where he had put it. In the center of the earth floor was a big, flat-topped stone whose roots seemed to go so far down that it was certain the cabin had been built around it. An amusing trick for a fellow to build a house around a natural table. And still there was the low, hand-made stool that that unknown owner had made for himself. Perhaps he often had taken it, as Tommy Grant did now, into the open, and sat with his back to the cabin wall, while he looked out across the two worlds of heaven and earth, to where they met in the dark, uneven horizon of the west.

Brownie came over and grazed close to him. He laid his hand gently on the tender flank of the colt and felt the skin twitch a little under his fingers. It made him laugh, and the laughter filled his throat and seemed to stay there.

He was hungry. When he thought of his hunger, such a wave of lonely desolation swept over him that he had to set his teeth and brace his will for the thinking of other thoughts. He tightened his belt a notch. The old-timers always said that this was a help, and now it would have to be a comfort to Tommy. A man can go three days without food, he remembered. Yes, three days without food or water. He made a cigarette and lighted it.

Suppose that a rifleman lay yonder at the black edge of the woods and used that light for the sighting of his gun?

"Bah!" Tommy said aloud, and held the match up above his head until it singed the ends of his fingers. A wolf that trembles at every "if" in life must die young, and he was a wolf, now, outcast from the flocks. People would speak of him, hereafter, as he himself had spoken for years of such fellows as Lefty Hilton, and Bert Ellis— with little icy tremors that shot up the back to the base of the brain. When one is in the wilderness, one has to risk danger and trust the wilderness itself! He would trust it. He was ready for that.

He smoked and found comfort. He forgot his hunger as he listened to the wind murmuring in a friendly manner among the trees. Brownie grazed always close beside him. There was only one thing on earth to which his attention was tied from this height, and that was to Margie.

Suppose that they caught him and shot him to death or hanged him. Well, Margie would never forget. She would go to his grave. Or suppose that when he was caught, they merely called it manslaughter, or some such thing? Suppose that they let him out in eight or ten years for good behavior. Well, Margie would be waiting. Even fellows like Sid Levine had been able to see in her the noblest virtue of all. Even the dead man must have been drawn by faith more than beauty.

It grew colder momentarily.

He went in and lay on the pile of pine boughs. They were soft enough, but heat which the cabin had hoarded up from the day had seeped out rapidly and he saw that he would not be able to sleep without covering. He decided, therefore, to build a fire inside the cabin, warm himself thoroughly, and then slip into the stack of boughs, making of them both a bed and a bed covering. Afterward, no doubt, if he avoided the law long enough, he would grow as thick skinned as a horse, and cold would make small difference to him.

He got up, made the fire, and watched with concern, until he saw that the rents in the roof were acting perfectly as a chimney to draw off the masses of smoke. The upper part of the cabin filled with a dense white fog into which the draft reached and snatched out armfuls of the mist. He divided the fire into two small heaps and sat between them, soaking up the heat.

He knew no one was apt to see that light. The cabin hooded it on three sides, and on the fourth the dull rays that wandered through the doorway were high above the level of any seeking eye.

Brownie came to the door and looked in. The firelight danced in his eyes. He sniffed at the smoke with shuddering nostrils and shook his head.

Tommy laughed.

"Come on, boy," he said.

Brownie stepped in, cautiously, snorting as though he found the earth uneasy beneath his feet. And then, with a grunt such as a spur will bring from a horse, he whirled about and faced the door suddenly.

A man stood there, leaning a hand against the jamb. From the other hand, the light dripped down the long barrel of a Colt.

"Hello, kid," the man said. "Comfortable in here?"

VII

Sinister, ugly, evil was the face that looked down the gun barrel at Tommy Grant. It was a face easy to draw, with words or pencil, and it had been drawn often enough in both ways, for it was nearly all the great receding slope of the forehead, continued by the long downward sweep of the nose. The eyes were spotted in as bright points, and little space was left for the lips, while the chin was pushed up close to the nose. There are deep sea fish that have such a look. Wind burn and sunburn had turned his skin to leather that was deeply wrinkled at the corners of the eyes.

That was Lefty Lew Hilton. That was the shadow that had risen outside the window and shot Bert Ellis to death, but one could feel that he needed to use no subterfuge, for how could such hands and such eyes fail in a gunfight.

He wore a canvas coat, blackened by grease stains, and leather trousers that bunched into great bags around the knees. Vanity appeared only in his boots, glove-like in texture and in fit. The toe of the right boot had been horribly torn. There was a loose flap of leather.

"Yeah. Pretty comfortable," breathed Tommy Grant.

"Got a gun on you?"

"Yeah," said Tommy, after a pause.

"Where?"

"Under my jacket."

"Spill it on the ground."

The muzzle of Lefty's revolver twitched up. His pose remained as loose and careless as ever, and it seemed that the gun and the gun hand alone were vigilant while Tommy Grant pulled out his own weapon. A brave and adroit man would use that instant to plant a fatal bullet in the body of Hilton, but the mere thought of such an attempt made Tommy grow faint. He laid his Colt on the earthen floor.

Hilton picked it up and made it disappear in amongst his clothes. His own gun was also out of sight. He made a cigarette, never glancing at the work of his hands.

"So you went and bumped off Bert Ellis?" asked Lefty.

Tommy Grant swallowed. He felt the bulge of his eyes as he stared up at the other.

"You went and bumped him off, eh?" Lefty repeated.

Tommy swallowed again. Some answer should be made, but what answer would be acceptable?

"No," he said at last.

"Oh, you didn't, eh?"

"No. Mind if I make a cigarette?"

"Why should I mind?"

"I don't know. Maybe you'd think . . . I don't know."

"Go on. Tell me why I should mind."

"If I started to make a move, reaching for something . . ."

Tommy's painfully staring eyes saw a smile appear between the nose and the chin of Lefty. It kept growing until it became prodigious. The lower lip curled out against the chin.

"I'd be scared of a lightnin' gunplay, eh?" Lefty asked with a grin.

"I don't know."

"You can build yourself a cigarette, kid."

He strode across the room suddenly and sat on the stone table. Brownie, with a snort, jumped for the door and disappeared, while Tommy stood up from between the fires.

Lefty pointed with his cigarette, but the boy stood transfixed.

"You know me, kid?"

"No."

"Never seen me before?"

"No."

"You lie!" Lefty thundered.

Tommy drew in a long breath.

"You lie. You know me. Tell me my name."

"Maybe you're Lefty Hilton."

The man nodded, slowly considering Tommy. His eyes seemed too small for expression. They were merely two points of brightness and darkness intermingled, and yet evil waxed and waned in them constantly.

"You only could guess that, eh? You wouldn't know for sure, kid?"

"You're Lefty Hilton," said the boy.

"Too bad you didn't bump off Bert Ellis. I could like the man that socked that gent. You know what he was?"

"No," said the boy.

"He was a damned skunk. You know what else he was?"

"No."

"He was a dirty sneak, and a double-crossin' washout, but mostly he was a damned heartbreaker. You hear me?"

"Yes."

"What does a woman go by?"

"I don't know."

"Want me to tell you?"

"All right."

"Lingo is all she goes by. Has a guy got a lingo? That's all she wants. It don't matter how much man he is. Look at Bert. All he had was a lingo. It was his lingo and his brown eyes. He was a snake, but he had eyes like a calf, when he wanted to. It was his lingo and his eyes. Damn him! That's what done it. I knew a girl . . ."

His glance shifted toward the open door, where he looked not into the darkness but into a vision from the past.

"So you didn't kill Bert?" he went on.

"No."

"Who did?"

"I don't know."

"Do you guess, though?"

"Yes. I guess."

"Well, who?"

"You killed Ellis."

Between nose and chin, the grin of Lefty grew once more and made his face more horrible than before.

"I killed Ellis, did I?"

"I think so."

"I killed him," agreed Lefty. "But you know somethin'?"

"No."

"I'm sorry."

He paused a little, gripped both his hands, and made his eyes disappear in a squint of fury.

"I'm sorry that I didn't have a chance to eat his heart. That's what I wanted . . . to eat his heart."

Trouble grew darker and darker in the mind of Tommy Grant, for criminals are not apt to confess their crimes to people who may be able to repeat the story. He was almost relieved when the other enlarged on the subject.

"But nobody's ever gonna believe that I killed him. Not now. You take a sheriff like Purvis, he's a bloodhound. Throw a scent up his nose, and he'll never leave the trail. He'll never change. He ain't got the sense to change."

He began to laugh, his head and shoulders shaking up and down. As his mouth gaped with mirth, he looked like a hideous half-wit.

"For Purvis, you're the gent that bumped off Bert Ellis. You're the one. He started after you and he hunted you. He'll never change. God Almighty couldn't tell him that anybody but you done that killin'. He'll get you and he'll hang you for that job. It's funny, ain't it? I gotta laugh when I think of you hangin' for that sort of a job. You!"

He laughed again. "How'd you get away?" he asked curiously.

"I jumped through the doorway. They didn't seem to think I'd try to move. But I managed to jump through the doorway, and lock the door behind me. That gave me a start."

"There was so many of 'em that they all thought they had you," Lefty told Tommy Grant. "It ain't twenty men that kills a bear, though. It's one man that knows he's gonna do the trick. You wouldn't've got loose from Purvis by himself. You got loose from him because the others gummed things up."

He made another cigarette.

"Got any chuck with you?" he asked Tommy.

"No."

"Can't you say nothin' but yes or no, you

dummy?" shouted Lefty. "You're a damned dummy, is what you are. You ain't got nothing to eat on you."

"Not a bite."

"That's hell," growled Lefty. "Whatcha mean by comin' away without nothin'? Don't you know nothin' about travelin' around? You ain't got nothin'."

"No."

"The 'no' boy, is what you are. Nothin' but 'no' is what a man can get out of you. Ain't you got no education? How far'd you go in school?"

"High school."

"High school, eh?"

"Yes."

"He said 'yes.' He can say somethin' besides 'no.' He's wonderful. He went to high school, and that's why he's got so many words. Listen, kid. You go all the way through high school?"

"Yes."

"Look here!"

"Yes."

"You mean to say that you went right on and graduated from high school?"

"Yes."

"You're a high school graduate, are you? You're one of them educated gents, are you?"

"No. I don't know much."

"No, you don't know *very* much," sneered Lefty. "Books is a waste of time. All the worst dummies, they been to school. They're all like you. They don't know nothin'. Except how to shoot the moon!"

His bad humor left him suddenly and he laughed again, more heartily than ever.

"I just stood there outside the window quite a spell, lookin' in and laughin'. I had Bert in the hollow of my hand. I stood there and laughed and laughed, holdin' him, ready to pop him off any second, and watchin' a kid like you shoot the moon, and trim him. Till he got crooked. I had to laugh, seein' an educated high school dummy like you that sat there right opposite to Bert Ellis and shot the moon, and made a fool out of Bert. That's what made me laugh. Bert that was goin' after your girl, when he'd trimmed you . . . I just had to stand and laugh."

It blurred the mind of Tommy to think of the murderer outside the window, laughing, but what was most amazing was that the danger had come upon him because of Margie.

"How did you find this place? How did you find me, Lefty?" he asked.

"You're my luck, kid," grinned Lefty. "That's how I come to find you. I found my luck. That's all. You can't part me from my luck. I'm sure to come to it. When you led the gang out of town, I drifted along behind. You cleared the way for me and I just followed.

"Then, back in the woods, my horse went dead

lame, and when I thought a minute, I remembered this here place. I peeled the saddle and bridle off it, and started to walk. Then I seen the glint of the fire in the trees, and put down what I was luggin', and soft-footed till I got to the door."

"You knew about this place? That's queer."

"No, it ain't queer. I know all about the hang-outs all around this neck of the woods. It's my range, and I know it."

The darkness outside of the door had been momentarily lightening, and now it was possible to see the tree tops that rose above the shoulder of the mountain. The moon was well up.

"There's only one thing," murmured Tommy Grant.

"What's the one thing, kid?"

"Suppose that they stay around, hunting for me. . . ."

"Oh, they'll stay around, all right. Old Purvis, he's got the scent and he won't leave the trail yet . . . not for a while."

"But suppose that they find the horse you left? Won't they begin cutting for sign from that point?"

"Yeah, it's likely that they will."

Tommy gasped: "But then they're likely to get to this place before . . ."

"Yeah, they're likely to get here. But what do I care? They can work as hard as they want . . . so long as I've got the brown colt."

"So long as you've got what?"

The face of Lefty twisted with malice.

"Did you think that I aimed to walk, you fool, with a man's horse like the brown goin' to waste on *you?*"

VIII

At the door, Lefty paused to say: "You stop me from the colt. You shoot the moon and stop me, kid, if you can."

Tommy moistened his lips, but no words came. Through such a veil as that which hangs before the eyes of a man newly wakened from sleep, he stared at Brownie, as the colt was caught and bridled by the ruffian. The horse danced and threw up its head. Lefty cursed it heartily. Trembling, the brown stood fast, wincing when the saddle was flopped on its back. Its frightened eyes glistened as they rolled toward the master who stood inert by the cabin and saw the accomplishment of the theft.

It was not only the horse that was being stolen, but all the hardness of four years, every cheerful moment, and the joy that had followed him day and night as the colt grew to the fulfillment of every early promise. For four years he had dreamed happily of what the brown might be. For four years he had seen his dreams realized.

Something rose up savagely in him, set his teeth, burned in his eyes—and then slowly dissipated like smoke in the wind of his fears. For that was Lew Hilton, who stood yonder pulling up the cinches with a brutal force that made the brown horse grunt and stagger.

He looked down, and saw the glint of the spurs, and the long spoon-handle bend of them. They were real Mexican spurs, and with them Lefty was famous for finding the last spark of life in his mount. It was said by the mountaineers that when a white man had abandoned a horse as useless, a Mexican still could get a day's work out of the bronco, an Indian could ride it another three days when the Mexican cast it into the discard, and that the tortured wreck of the beast would still serve that cruel fiend Lefty Hilton for a week.

Tommy Grant moaned, as though the spurs were already buried in his own flanks when he saw the outlaw swing into the saddle. Brownie was reined sharply away, switching his tail in a mild protest against the roughness of the hand that controlled him. Electric points of pain came prickling out in the forehead of Tommy.

Brave men die once—cowards many times. Who had said that? And like the passing of his own soul, he saw the gleaming, polished body of the colt pass out of the moonlight into the shadow of the woods. Instantly, not space, but grisly years of sorrow separated them.

The sound of his own voice startled him. He was shouting, calling, running blindly forward. Something exploded in the brush. Branches snapped, and Lefty Hilton, that famous rider, cursed loudly. Then Brownie was returning, fighting his head against the restraint of the curb which his silken mouth had never felt before. He pitched here and there like a ship in a cross sea among the shadows, but broke away at last toward his master, as a long branch stretched from the side and with an easy gesture, as it seemed, brushed Hilton from the saddle. Brownie came on like a gallop. The bridle reins flickered above his head. The stirrups leaped at his side. Hope and happiness came toward the boy in the empty saddle.

He raised his hand but, even without that command, Brownie was coming to a halt. Now his left hand gathered the reins and the tuft of mane at the withers, his left foot was lifted for the stirrup. In an instant he would be in flight across the mountains like a wild hawk, but then he heard the brief, deep note of a revolver. With a hammer stroke and a knife thrust, a bullet drove through his right thigh between knee and hip. The pain was in his body and burning in his brain as he fell flat.

Across the clearing, he saw Hilton racing toward him, leaning far forward, with a poised revolver held like a lantern as high as his head. The gun spoke, Tommy fell flat on his face again, paralyzed by fear, though without a second wound. He was hurt, and he would be murdered, but it was more than fear of death that enthralled him as Hilton came nearer.

Perhaps he would have lain there inert, numb with horror as some poor worm that has been poisoned by the wasp's sting, but in falling his right hand had dropped on the ragged face of a stone. That was what put the hope of resistance in his mind. He gripped it hard in the ecstasy of his terror, and the stone came free from the soil.

Hilton was near. His footfalls beat upon the ground. Curses crowded the other words on his lips, but he was saying that he would give Tommy a foretaste of hell, and then send him there for a full meal. It was something like that, panting and spluttering forth.

Tommy lifted himself on hand and knee with the rock heaved up in his hand. Hilton was too near to check himself. He tried a snap shot that missed—and then the flung rock caught him full in the face. The gun flung to the side, slithering away through the grass as Lefty staggered, both hands at his face. Tommy caught those uncertain legs in both arms and the weight of the big fellow crashed down upon him. One elbow hit the wounded thigh. Fire, nauseating agony poured through the vitals of Tommy, yet he twisted himself about and grappled with the arms of Lefty Lew.

"I'm gonna scalp you. I'm gonna make a redhead out of you. I'm gonna burn you alive!" yelled Hilton. "You . . ."

His face was streaming blood. He jerked a hand free and hammered his fist against Tommy's head, but the blow seemed no more than a shadowy gesture. Neither pain nor a stunning shock grappled the mind of the boy. He was amazed.

The hand rose again He caught it in mid-air—and held it.

Twice and again, Hilton strove to drive the punch home or to tear his wrist free, but the grip of the boy was firmly glued. The hope was first born in Tommy, hope, and a savage eagerness.

That wrist was abandoned to him as, with his other hand, Lefty snatched out a second gun. The gun hand was caught in turn, imprisoned, frozen into a vice.

"My God!" groaned Lefty, and in a frenzy struggled until they turned over and over on the ground, every turn a grinding agony to the boy, as the double weight fell upon his wound. Half his side was wet, slimy with his own blood.

"I'm dying!" he yelled at Lefty. "But I'm going to kill you first. I'm going to . . . strangle you . . . you devil!"

One hand of Lefty came suddenly free as they writhed. The very stone that had been hurled into his face he caught up by a sheer chance and struck Tommy over the head with it.

"Take that! And that . . ."

The edges of the stone bit like teeth into the skull of the boy. He saw the armed hand lifted high again, the moon blazed with dazzling brilliance against his eyes, but he managed to strike his elbow into the dripping mask of Lefty.

The stone fell idly to the ground as they grappled again.

Now the boy could bless the patient years of his labor which had clothed his shoulders with strength and given him hands of iron. The power of Lefty Hilton was a tiger's, fit for a leap and a stroke but not for this prolonged struggle, body to body.

"I'm going to kill you!" snarled Tommy. "I'm going to kill you! I'm going to strangle you!"

A trumpet sounded deafeningly above him— the brown colt, neighing frantically as he saw his master struggling, and smelled the human blood. Off to the edge of the mountain shoulder fled the brown, wavered on the edge of the tree shadows, and then came hurrying back while the peal of his neighing rang across the mountain night.

The breathing of Lefty was a hoarse, broken gasp. A shudder took his body, and increased in violence, but still his spirit was great to make a final effort that raised them both to their feet, that spun them about, and jerked him free, at last. The whole sleeve of his coat came away like torn paper in the terrible grasp of the boy, but there was Lefty rushing with outstretched hand toward a glitter of steel in the grass.

The right leg of the boy was almost useless, so from the left alone he sprang forward. The uttermost reach of his fingertips brushed vainly on the hip of Hilton, and then, as he struck the ground at full length, his clutch fell on an ankle. The grip was broken as soon as it was made, but the wrench that resulted was sufficient to knock Lefty off balance. He toppled, beating the air with both arms as though they were wings. He fell, tumbling head over heels.

But as Tommy lifted himself with a frantic haste, he saw that the sure hand of the outlaw had found the gun.

Off one knee, off both hands, he leaped as a lamed cat might spring, and flung himself on the other. That gun, that gleaming little instrument of death was his target, and as his hand closed over the fingers of Hilton, the weapon was inside the double grip.

The knee of Lefty caught him in the ribs, raking away the skin, grinding the flesh against the bones, knocking the breath from his body like the kick of a horse. From that moment he was as one struggling under water, deprived of the power of breathing but forced to fight for his life.

Panic made him tremble. In that instant of appalling fear he felt the hand of Lefty turning the gun toward him. All his might was needed to

203

check the movement, to start the hand of Lefty turning toward Lefty's body.

He was underneath now. Then as Lefty fiercely struggled for freedom, they lay on their sides, his right hand on Hilton's left that held the gun, his thumb over Lefty's trigger finger. Strangulation was in the boy's throat. His lungs labored for air and found none. His mouth opened and shut like that of a gasping fish. His eyes bulged until the moon became a blur and the face of Lefty disappeared, but still he was bending the gun in toward the body of the other when pain cut into his shoulder—Lefty, like a frantic beast, had sunk his teeth in the flesh.

The gun could be moved no more. It had reached the body of Lefty, then, and could not be stirred, but where it pointed, the boy could not tell.

His lungs were on fire, now. He could not endure another instant when he drove his thumb hard down on the resisting finger of Lefty. The gun boomed. The whole body of Hilton turned to water and flattened gradually on its back.

At that instant, it was possible for Tommy Grant to breathe a groan with every labor of his lungs, and he sat up to stare at the horribly disfigured face of Hilton. On his side was a red welter. His eyes stared at the moon. His mouth gaped.

From the wound in Tommy's head, blood trickled over his face. He put up a hand and wiped the current away. His fingers were dark in the moon shine with the fluid. But in place of the strength he had lost, there was a new power flowing through his body. He felt no joy of victory. He had been man enough to master Hilton, but for that matter he did not often meet his match pitching hay or lifting bales. It was not strange that he had been able to deal with Hilton, hand to hand, but what quickened the heart of Tommy Grant was the sense that good fortune followed him. From the trap of Bert Ellis, from the pursuit of the sheriff's posse, from this last and more dreadful danger of Lefty Lew, he had managed to escape. He wondered why no tremors ran through him, why a singular calm possessed him. No explanation was possible, except that he felt his luck, and entrusted himself to it.

Hilton lay there—dead, it seemed—with a bullet from his own gun in his body. Luck had done that, luck had beaten Lefty—and the good brown horse had saved Tommy Grant.

He fell to work bandaging the wound in his leg, for the cold of the night air was making it ache with a pulse that constantly increased. He pulled off his overalls, slit the right leg of the trousers into lengths, and then reached for the clothes of Hilton.

Something stopped his hand. He was sure that Lefty was dead, but still he could not use the cloth of that shirt. Instead, he stripped off his own shirt and undershirt and built the bandage carefully, first laying on a quantity of dust to check the flow of the blood. It was a narrow puncture through which the bullet had entered, but the spot where it issued was a horrible gap. He stuffed them both with dust, pausing once until a wave of nausea diminished. Even if he did not bleed to death, suppose that blood poisoning set in?

The arm on which he leaned, sagged and shuddered at the elbow. Over the dust pads, he built the bandage, winding it tightly so that the wounds were gripped harder and harder. All the nerves of his body seemed to be gathered there where the bandages gripped their raw surfaces, but he knew that there was no other way to check the fatal drain.

He pulled on the overalls again, wriggling into the one remaining leg painfully, and it was as he pulled his belt tight that he heard a voice call among the trees below the shoulder of the hill.

He forgot his torment. His brain cleared instantly as he rose to one knee.

Out of the distance a second voice answered the first, and then he heard a crackling among the shrubbery close by. It meant that he had short seconds left to him if he were to get away. No doubt they had found Lefty's crippled horse; no doubt they had been guided from that place by the noise of the guns. At any rate, here they were upon him. They could not be other than the sheriff's men!

The brown colt, like one skirmishing in a fight, had been drawing near to his master, then springing away from the horrible smell of blood, but now he came straight up to and stood by him faithfully, though his legs were trembling while the boy caught the stirrup, then the stirrup leather, the pommel and cantle, and sprang up from one leg. He struck heavily against the side of the horse and full on the outer wound in his leg.

Exquisite torture made him groan. He shut his teeth and crowded the voice back as it rose in his throat, then pulled himself higher, caught his wounded leg with his hand, and dragged it over the cantle. Heavily he slumped down into the saddle. His dangling feet automatically found the stirrups, yet he had to remain there, paralyzed with the anguish, emotionless, his very brain at a halt, while he heard the footfalls draw nearer though the underbrush.

It was then that Lefty Hilton sat up with a groan, suddenly, and then rose to his feet. It was like seeing the dead walk, and so a newly restored strength might have operated, letting Hilton move with a stagger toward his enemy. He was dying on his feet. Hatred took the place of breath and heart in him.

The horror of it restored Tommy a little. He

was able to rein the colt away into the shadows of the trees. Looking back from them, he saw Lefty tottering in pursuit with blind hands stretched out to find the way, while from the brink of the opposite woods, three men appeared, on the run.

That was all he saw. He heard them shout. A rapid fire of bullets rattled among the branches of the trees about him, but Brownie was already sliding and slipping down the shoulder of the mountain, deep in the woods, while his master gripped the pommel with both hands, and prayed for strength to endure.

Still the noises from above followed Tommy Grant.

He heard the voice of the sheriff shout a command to halt. He heard Lefty Hilton yell a defiance. Then there was more gunfire.

He gasped as he heard it. Were they shooting down that shambling helpless wreck of a man?

All the world was filled with brutality. There was only the colt . . . and Margie.

It was only a miracle that kept Tommy on the horse. He grew dizzy. The waves of darkness and of moonlight, silver clear, made his brain spin. It was impossible for him to guide the brown. He could only cling with both hands, his mouth working as the sick weakness mounted in his breast.

This lasted not minutes or hours, but through eternal stretches of time and space until at last he was aware that they had issued from the woods and were moving through the rolling foothills. He looked above, to the ridges of the mountains. They seemed a black wave leaning out to topple on him, so he closed his eyes, bent his head, and let the colt go on at his own will.

IX

He came to a grayness of time and place, when the country around him was dimly familiar, and the light of the moon was weak, though still the battered globe of it stood well above the horizon. It was not greatly past the full phase, and therefore the feebleness of the illumination amazed Tommy. He stared with wide, uncomprehending eyes at the sky. The senses of men fail, he knew, just before death comes to them. Death, therefore, must be at his side!

That was not strange, for he was sure that the torture he endured was enough in itself to kill him. His leg was now numb from the hip down, but from the upper surface of that numbness, shooting pains thrust into his body, lance heads of agony that found the heart with every pulse of his blood. He wondered that any life remained to him. It was as though a man should keep his existence after being transfixed a thousand times with sharp steel.

Brownie went on wearily, head down, but with never a stumble. The boy spoke, and instantly the ears pricked forward, the head lifted and turned a little.

A sudden hope came to Tommy Grant that the fortune which had helped him through the last day would keep with him now and let him remain in the saddle until he fell dead from it. That would be far better than to slip weakly to the earth and lie there by hours and hours, kept from unconsciousness by the pain he endured. Yet he felt that he must soon fall.

He looked about him on the country where he was to end his life. To the left were easily rolling fields. To the right was land freshly furrowed, with a gang-plow standing in the center of the unfinished section. Beside the road was a tree whose head had been broken off by an old storm, and now hung down lifelessly along the lower trunk.

That tree caused him to frown with wonder, and shake his head. For it seemed familiar. It was lodged somewhere in his memory together with familiar events of everyday life. Either in dreams or in facts, he seemed to have seen it many times before. Indeed, the very road seemed known to him, and he had seen what lay on the farther side of the hill over which it now disappeared. Surely he knew what was there, if only he could bring it to mind. But illusions like this, no doubt, were common among people who were at the end of the trail.

He looked down at the ditch beside the road. If he fell from the saddle, probably he would roll weakly down the slope and lie half in the water and the mud. There they would find him. Perhaps his body would be taken to Fruit Dale. Perhaps they would send word to the ranch, and there Margie would dress herself in her best clothes to go to town. She would put on the gray woolen skirt, the blue blouse, the short gray jacket, the hat that had the downy tuft of yellow feathers at the side. Over the hands that were her vanity, she would draw gloves of delicately soft leather, and so she would set forth with her face pale and her eyes widened by terror.

Thinking of that, he forgot his misery and even smiled a little. The dried blood on his face cracked, and resisted the smile.

He stared about him again, wondering why this scene appeared so familiar. But now he saw that the hills to the east were inky black against a horizon rather gray than silver-lighted by the moon. It was the exact duplication of early dawn. Dawn, in fact, it was.

That was why the moon appeared dull. That was why the wind turned his naked leg blue, above and below the bandage, and kept him shuddering. For autumn mornings come coldly over the earth. His shirt and undershirt had been used in making the bandage. The jacket of his overall was as chilly as a coat of mail, and rasped against his skin.

The colt began to press forward suddenly, as he reached the slope on which the road wound, and still those windings appeared familiar, the very ruts were printed in the mind of Tommy Grant as though he had seen them a thousand times before.

Through that dream he reached the top of the hill, restraining the eagerness of the colt with a hoarse murmur, but as they gained the easy summit, he cried out in wonder. In a trice all the mystery was stripped from the scene. His bewildered brain mastered everything at a stroke. For yonder in the hollow lay the sheds, the barn, the weak-backed house of Sylvester Train.

He checked the colt, and sat the saddle, staring. His weakness seemed to be stricken from him. The very pain of his wounds diminished and now as a curling wisp, and then a thick cloud of smoke broke from the top of the kitchen chimney, he laughed a little, and let Brownie go on.

Margie was down there, at work. She had stuffed the firebox of the stove and now the paper had ignited, the flames and smoke were rushing upward, and coils of white mist were working through the air of the room. Instantly he could breathe more easily. Peace came on his mind and power on his body. At a stride he was far from the fear of death.

He rode down straight to the kitchen door. Out in the barn, one of the horses whinnied with a deep, rasping note. That would be the old gray.

No, he remembered that the horses were not there, unless someone else had driven them out from the town. No, it was the bay mare with the sore shoulder, lonely in the big barn, and calling for her master and for her mates.

As he drew nearer to the house, he saw that the windmill had been allowed to run all night, so that the water troughs were overflowed and the ground about them was a small lake. Still the big wheel spun in the morning wind and the pump clanked and the water sparkled in rhythmic bursts from the end of the pipe.

Well, they would miss him on this place. In the four years of his stay, such carelessness had never been seen.

He took his bare right leg under the knee and lifted the numb weight of it over the cantle, shook his left foot from the stirrup, slid cautiously down to the ground. Brownie turned a weary head, wave-marked with the dried salt of sweat, and sniffed at him, still frightened by the smell of blood. But Tommy Grant turned to the door of the kitchen, hopping on his left leg, the right foot dragging. Two years ago the greyhound had broken a foreleg and come in dragging the foot like this, Tommy remembered. Sylvester Train had shot the poor dog, and Tommy had buried it.

He turned the knob of the door, pressed it open, and hopped in to confront Margie. She was between the stove and the window. The lamp shone down on the white of the well-scrubbed floor, on the old shoes she wore, on the clean apron with which she began every day's work. It

215

glinted, also, on a pair of rubber gloves. But the upper part of her body was in shadow, her face was a blur.

He closed the door behind him and braced an arm against the wall. A foolish smile twisted his face until the drying blood crackled.

"You know, Margie . . . I got the gloves for you, but I left them behind . . . in Fruit Dale."

He had to say something. That was better than standing mute. Now she ran suddenly to him. She put her hands against his breast, as though to help support his weight. He was aware of the whiteness of her face, of the fragrance that always faintly surrounded her, like that which issues on the opening of a drawer where lavender had been kept to sweeten the clothes.

"The team ran away, Tommy. You've been in a smash. Your leg . . . it looks to be broken!"

It appeared difficult and unprofitable to explain.

"No, it's not broken. I'll sit down here a minute."

He reached for a chair and dragged it nearer.

"You'll go to bed. I'll call Uncle Sylvester. You've got to get into bed. . . ."

He broke in and silenced her with the weight of a few words.

"I'm only going to rest here, a minute. They'll be after me," he said.

It was exactly as though he had struck her

216

in the face. Her head went back and her body shuddered.

"That old bathrobe upstairs. You get it for me, Margie, will you? I'm sort of cold."

He lowered himself into the chair, as he spoke, closing his eyes, sighing with infinite relief as he settled his shoulders and head against the wall. It seemed as though a weight had been tied to his head, pulling it forward, and now that strain was relieved. When he opened his eyes, he saw that she was gone.

"Margie! Oh, Margie," called the patient, enduring voice of Sylvester Train.

There was no answer.

"Mar-gie! Oh, Margie!" repeated the voice.

"Y-e-e-s!" came the answer of the girl, trailing swiftly toward the kitchen.

He heard the footfalls coming, strangely light and noiseless, though there was a faint tremor running through the house at the same time.

She came, the bathrobe flinging behind with the speed of her running.

Tommy Grant sat up. The desperate brightness of her eyes frightened him as she pulled the robe over his shoulders.

"I'm all right," he assured her. "Only I'm cold . . . a little. As soon as I'm warmed up, I'll start on . . ."

"Of course you're all right," said the girl. She was on her knees, her glance searching his face, her hands traveling over the red surfaces of the bandage with anxious inquiry. "What did it, Tommy?"

"It's all right," said Tommy. "I only want to rest."

"Lean back, then, and rest," she said.

"All right, for a minute."

She got a knife from the table and slit the bandage across, then unwound it rapidly. It came off in stiff half cylinders, with the dark bloodstains permeating each, the spots widening from the top toward the bottom.

She was saying: "Who is after you . . . who is hunting you, Tommy?"

"I don't know. The sheriff . . . a posse. I don't know who else."

He looked toward the ceiling. The warmth of the kitchen bathed his body in dreamy ease and content, except for the torment of the scalp wound and the band of icy pain that froze his flesh to the bone of his leg. But the nearness of Margie and the warmth of the kitchen and the familiarity of the room oddly balanced against the anguish of the wounds. He fitted his shoulders more comfortably against the wall. If his head slipped to the side at an angle, he wondered if there would be in his neck sufficient strength to straighten it again.

"Sheriff Purvis?"

"Yes. The sheriff. And a lot of others."

"What have you done?"

He heard the words, and contemplated the long course of action as it arose mistily in his thoughts. Then he shook his head, for the answer would require too many words.

The last of the bandage was unwound. It revealed the blueness of his swelling leg, it left a deep impression, perfectly white, as though invisible hands were gripping his flesh. He rocked his head forward to view the thing and wondered at the small mouths of the wounds that had tortured him like the tearing fangs of a wolf. Blood oozed from them in a thin dribble.

"It's all right," said Tommy.

"Margie!" shouted Sylvester Train in a sudden fury.

They could hear him lifting himself from his bed, and the heavy stamping of his feet on the floor.

Tommy Grant quailed as he listened.

"Train is going to make trouble. You'd better fix his coffee," said Tommy. "He'll be pretty hot. Call to him, Margie."

She held her hands on either side of the bleeding leg, as though she were about to close them over the mouths of the wound, and fiercely she looked up at his face.

"Are you afraid of him?" she asked through her teeth.

"I guess I am," said Tommy.

219

"*I'm* not!" she answered. "I want him to make trouble. I want him to make it."

"Do you?" muttered the boy. "My Lord, Margie, you look as though you mean it."

There was more stamping in the distance as Sylvester Train stamped his feet home into his boots, sending a slight quiver through the flimsy house.

"I've got to be going on . . . you'd better put the bandage back on. I've got to start before they . . ."

She stood before him. He watched the rapid rise and fall of her breast.

"You're going to sit there till I've washed that leg and bandaged it again. Then you're going to bed," she declared.

"Look, Margie," he explained, "I can't do that. You know how it is. I can't do that. I've got to . . ."

"Be still!"

She was already pouring steaming water from the kettle into the brightly burnished dish pan. This she tempered with a liberal splash from the bucket that stood in the sink, but the steaming still arose from the mixture. She dropped a clean rag into it and laid the pan on the floor. The rag she soused once or twice as she kneeled, felt the heat of it by touching it against her bare elbow, and then held it above his leg. Frowningly, she looked in his face to observe the effect as she squeezed a trickle from the cloth.

The warmth penetrated slowly through the cold, through the agony. It was a thawing of a long winter of distress. Tommy Grant, shuddering with relief, laughed foolishly, weakly.

Then as she began to swab the leg, big Sylvester Train strode into the room with an Olympian frown on his brow.

"Margie, did you hear me call?" he thundered.

The reverberations of his voice ran through every nerve of Tommy Grant, but Train saw the hurt man, now, and grunted loudly under the shock of the surprise.

"What's this?" he demanded, pointing at the wounds and the blood-stained water in the pan. Instantly his thought reverted to his own interests.

"Where's the team? I didn't hear the wagons come up the road. I didn't hear them on the bridge. What brought you here?"

"Brownie," said Tommy.

"And the team. Where's the team?"

"I left them in Fruit Dale . . . Washington Street."

"Washington Street? You infernal, worthless, ignorant, thick-witted fool, what did you mean by leaving them back in Fruit Dale?"

"Stand out of the light!" said a sharp voice.

It was a moment before Tommy could realize that the girl was speaking.

"Are you talking to me, young lady?" said Sylvester Train. "Are you daring to lift . . . ?"

"I'm talking to you! Stand out of the light!" she cried. She pointed at him. "Move, will you?"

Sylvester Train stepped back, very much as one recoils before leaping forward. His heavy jowls bloated with passion.

"I demand to know what you . . . ," began Train.

"Answer him, Tommy," said the girl. "Or he'll still be talking. Uncle Sylvester . . . bring the hot water . . . the kettle."

Sylvester Train stared at her, hesitated, and then brought the kettle from the stove. In deep amazement, the boy watched him obey the command.

"I had to leave the team," Tommy said. "They were chasing me."

The girl began to add hot water, cautiously, to that which was in the pan.

"Who was chasing you?" shouted Train, his anger freshened by speech.

"Sheriff Purvis and a crowd. . . ."

"The sheriff!" exclaimed Train. "Why?"

"Because Bert Ellis was shot. They thought I did it."

"They thought," sneered Sylvester Train, "that a weak-hearted nincompoop like you would dare to stand before . . ."

"Yes, before ten like Bert Ellis!" cried the girl, jerking her head up.

"Hold your tongue," said her uncle. "And they chased you and shot you, eh?"

"No, that was Lefty Hilton."

"Stuff and nonsense!" exclaimed Train. "Bert Ellis . . . Lefty Hilton . . . why, even to see two such men as that in one day would wither you up. Bert Ellis and Lefty Hilton? What are you talking about? And my team . . ."

"Bert is dead. Lefty shot him," said the boy. "But the crowd chased me. I got up in the hills near the Pass. Lefty found me, and started to take Brownie. . . ."

He sighed, and shook his head, remembering the wild tangle of the fight. Vaguely he was aware that the girl and Sylvester Train were gaping at him.

"Well, he shot me first," Tommy explained slowly. "Then we fought. I got his gun away from him. I shot him through the body . . . and . . . that's all. I just rode home."

"You? You shot Hilton with his own gun?" muttered Sylvester Train.

He put out a hand and found the wall with it.

"Tommy, are you faint?" asked Margie.

His head had sunk back against the wall. He lifted it quickly.

"No, I'm all right. You've taken the pain away, Margie. It makes me a little sleepy."

It seemed to him that he had been speaking of the events of a dream.

"You killed Lefty Hilton?" repeated Sylvester Train. "With his own gun? Where is it?"

"It's here," Tommy said.

He drew it out from beneath the pit of his left arm, where the holster clung against his body.

"You can see the notches filed into the handle," Tommy said, and held it out.

"Put down that gun!" said a voice at the outer door.

It had opened while they spoke. The grizzled head and the stooped shoulders of Sheriff Purvis were in the doorway.

X

Sylvester Train had taken the gun. He held it out toward the sheriff in both of his fat hands, crying: "Take it, Sheriff! Take it! I'm well rid of the gun and the rascal that stole it. Take the gun, and take the man, too. As worthless a . . ."

Sheriff Purvis, having received the gun, lifted a hand which silenced Train.

Through the doorway behind the sheriff came a press of tired men, and the smell of sweating horses filled the room. These fellows were unshaven, haggard with weariness. They took off their hats because Margie was in the kitchen, and every head was powdered with dust below the line of the hatband. Most of them spoke to Margie, in low voices, but she paid no attention to them, for the sheriff was her main concern.

She faced him with her arms stiffened at her sides, her fists clenched.

"You can't take him," she told Purvis. "Look . . . if you try to make him ride, you'll kill him!"

"Ridden to death, or hanged . . . what's the difference?" demanded Sylvester Train.

At this, every man in the posse turned on the farmer and looked at him with curious eyes. But Tommy Grant looked at them, not at Train, for it seemed to him now that he had always known there was no mercy, no kindness in the fat man.

"I wanted that gun in case of . . . accidents," said Sheriff Purvis. "I didn't say anything about wanting Thomas Grant."

He gave the name a certain emphasis. He set it apart in his speech with a sort of grave flourish that made Tommy forget his pain and his fear and his weariness.

Margie no longer intervened between him and the man of the law, but, stepping back beside the chair, she slipped her arm around the shoulders of the boy, and waited. Against his face he felt the rapid hammering of her heart.

"Now, what's the meaning of this?" Sylvester Train demanded loudly.

All those men continued to stare at him. The sheriff took out a handkerchief and mopped his forehead, though there was no sign of sweat on it. He merely made a dusty smear across his face.

Then tall Joe Randall cleared his throat, shrugged his wide shoulders, and said: "Train, if I was you, I'd put Tom Grant to bed and treat him fine. But if you ain't gonna do that, then some of us will have to camp out here with him till he's well enough to travel. Only . . . if I was you, I'd do some thinking."

A gloomy murmur of assent arose from the others.

Train, bewildered, stared about him.

"What I want to know," he exclaimed in his deeply resonant voice, "is whether you're after a lawbreaker or not?"

Sheriff Purvis lifted his right hand in a gesture so quick that it flashed. He pointed his forefinger at Sylvester Train.

"We gave Thomas Grant a run because we thought he'd killed Bert Ellis . . . though maybe Bert deserved killing. Grant beat us to the tall timber. Lefty Hilton caught up with him there. They fought and Hilton wounded him. He left Hilton dying. Lew confessed before he cashed in that *he* had shot Ellis. Boasted about it, in fact, and cursed because his gun was gone, and he couldn't file another notch into it. After Lefty died, we worked down the trail to your house, Train. When we come in here, we took off our hats because there's a brave man in here."

"My team of horses . . . ," muttered Sylvester Train. His voice went out and his eyes wandered from all those faces, and the contempt that curled their lips. He shrank . . . not backward, but in size. His head dropped as one who falls into a muse. From the depth of his present abasement, he knew that he would never recover, for too many people had been able to look in at the nakedness of his soul.

"You needn't carry him upstairs. Put him in my room," muttered Train, and went blundering across the floor and into the gray of the morning.

· · ·

So they bore Tommy Grant gently to the room of Train and stretched him on the big double bed with its lofty headpiece and the carved posts at its foot. In the disarray and poverty of the bare room its varnish glistened with a foolish pomp.

Sheriff Purvis helped with the re-bandaging of the leg. His skin was leather, but his touch was as soft as Margie's. His voice was hardly above a whisper as he assured the girl that all would be well, that the doctor would soon be there. Afterward, he stood at the bed for a moment, patting his hand.

"You're a lucky girl," Purvis said before he left.

All of these things were dimly perceived by Tommy Grant. The pain in his leg was gradually subsiding but a greater trouble gathered in his mind. Weakness flowed through him. His blood was water. He could only turn his hand palm up to beckon Margie. She sat on the bed beside him, leaning close, searching for his soul with her eyes, and finding it easily.

So he merely said: "You know, Margie. It's all a lot of bunk. About the brave man. I wasn't brave. Ellis scared me. I was afraid of Lefty Hilton, too. I was like a stone. And it's a terrible thing. People are going to think I'm a hero . . . or something. Then they'll find me out and despise me. I'm not a hero."

She was smiling, and this frightened him because he could not understand why she would smile.

"Are you despising me again, Margie?" he asked.

"No," said the whispering tremor of her voice. "I'm not despising you, Tommy."

A horse whinnied near the house, ending in a snort.

Tommy Grant sighed. "That's Brownie," he said. "I was so scared, that I would have left Hilton ride off on that colt. Only, at the last minute something made me call out. Brownie came back . . . the fight started . . . but I was only trying to get away. Everybody else is thinking big things about me, but all that ever saved me was luck and a horse. I wanted you to know."

The door pushed open with a sound like that of a drawn breath.

"Now, my lad," said the loud voice of Sylvester Train, entering, "just to show you that my heart's in the right place . . . just to cheer you up . . . I've brought a little present for you . . . all your back pay in one lump sum!"

He poured the gold pieces from one hand to the other in a bright stream, then with a sigh laid them in the fingers of Tommy, and stood back with a beaming face as one expecting applause.

But the two pairs of young eyes dwelt gravely and coldly on him. Not a word was uttered.

"What I thought . . . ," began Sylvester Train, faltering. "I mean to say . . . what I . . ."

He got to the door, mumbling like this, and suddenly fled like a child that fears company.

Margie looked back to Tommy and, dismissing Train from her mind, picked up the last thread of the conversation.

"I'll tell you what I know, Tommy . . . you're better than a hero," she said.

"What's better than a hero?" he asked rather faintly.

"Tommy Grant is," she answered.

"What do you mean?" Tommy asked. "Look, Margie . . . what are you crying about?"

"Because I'm so happy."

"It's no use. I'll never understand," Tommy said, and expelled a large sigh. "Look, Margie. There's Brownie. Look . . . he's found me again!"

The head of the colt was thrust through the open window. The wave-marks of dry salt were still on his face, but his ears pricked and his eyes glistened.

"Bless him," Margie said. "He's the only other one that understands."

"Understands what?" he asked.

"You," said Margie Train.

ABOUT THE AUTHOR

Max Brand is the best-known pen name of Frederick Faust, creator of Dr. Kildare, Destry, and many other fictional characters popular with readers and viewers worldwide. His enormous output, totaling approximately thirty million words or the equivalent of five hundred and thirty ordinary books, covered nearly every field: crime, fantasy, historical romance, espionage, Westerns, science fiction, adventure, animal stories, love, war, and fashionable society. Eighty motion pictures have been based on his works along with many radio and television programs. Perhaps no other author has reached more people in such a variety of different ways. Born in Seattle in 1892, orphaned early, Faust grew up in the rural San Joaquin Valley of California. At Berkeley he became a student rebel and one-man literary movement, contributing prodigiously to all campus publications. Denied a degree because of unconventional conduct, he embarked on a series of adventures culminating in New York City where, after a period of near starvation, he received simultaneous recognition as a serious poet and successful author of fiction. Later, he traveled widely, making his home in New York, then in Florence, Italy, and finally in Los Angeles. Once the United States entered the Second World

War, Faust abandoned his lucrative writing career and his work as a screenwriter to serve as a war correspondent with the infantry in Italy, despite his fifty-one years and a bad heart. He was killed during a night attack on a hilltop village held by the German army. New books based on magazine serials or unpublished manuscripts or restored versions continue to appear so that, alive or dead, he has averaged a new book every six months for seventy-five years. Beyond this, some work by him is newly reprinted every week of every year in one or another format somewhere in the world. A great deal more about this author and his work can be found in *The Max Brand Companion* (Greenwood Press, 1997) edited by Jon Tuska and Vicki Piekarski.

Center Point Large Print
600 Brooks Road / PO Box 1
Thorndike, ME 04986-0001 USA

(207) 568-3717

US & Canada:
1 800 929-9108
www.centerpointlargeprint.com